—BEYOND—
the DAINTREE

Destiny in Disguise Series

Book 3

— BEYOND —
the DAINTREE

Out of the Daintree to a New World

ANTHONY W BUIRCHELL

The novel is a historical fiction that takes place in the past and centres a plot on accurate details of the time in which it takes place. Historical fiction relies on real-life history to propel a novel or story's details and plot. The Author has used historical fiction to retell a historical event while changing minor details. The fiction often involves traditions and customs of previous periods, and it can include actual historical figures and settings.

 A catalogue record for this book is available from the National Library of Australia

National Library of Australia Cataloguing-in-Publication
Creator: Anthony William Buirchell
Title: Beyond the Daintree
Target Audience: Youth and adults.
Edition: 3rd edition.
ISBN: 9780975623008(paperback)
ISBN: 9780975623022(e-book)

Printed and Channel Distribution
Publishing Consultants Pickawoowoo Publishing Group

Publisher
Cric Croc Enterprises, www.criccroc.com.au
For inquiries, write to rights and permissions via publisher.
Lightning Source/ Ingram Australia

Other books by author Anthony W Buirchell
(Adults and Young Adult Readers)

Fiction:
Destiny in Disguise Series
Book 1 Destination Daintree
Book 2 Daintree Reflections
Book 3 Beyond the Daintree
Spirited Away (Published 2024)

Non Fiction:
The Restless Danish Immigrants – the Johnson
Family

Children's Books (Children from 0 to 8)
Cric Croc
Cric Croc and the Bedraggled Pony
Cric Croc and the Grate Rescue
Why Crocodiles Smile

Chapter 1

As a child, Max Johnson had grown up in the rainforest of the Daintree in Northern Queensland, Australia. Before the lumberjacks ventured into the area the Daintree was an untapped wilderness.

The timber cutters were in search of red cedar trees. They carved huge swathes through the jungle-like environment in their quest.

Each red cedar towered into the sky as straight as an arrow and their butts were wider than four men could encircle with arms out-stretched.

The work of swinging an axe into the trunks of these magnificent trees was backbreaking but lucrative. The lumberjacks kept their axes razor sharp and had a well-practiced swing that cut deep into the redwood with seemingly little effort. The axe head would penetrate to nearly the entire head depth and then with a flick of their wrists, the lumberjack would pull the axe out and swing with an uppercut movement below the first cut. The two cuts would meet and a large piece of wood would be ripped off. These constant movements soon had the trunk cut halfway through.

The axeman would then reverse himself going to the uphill side of the towering redwood and begin on that side. After an hour or so, a creaking sound grew louder, and to the lumberjack's acute hearing, he would step away and wait for gravity to do its share of the falling. The tree sheared off and fell downhill. As this began a yell of, "Timber," would echo across the hills warning all the other workers in the vicinity that a huge tree was toppling earthwards.

The logs were dragged by teams of horses or bullocks to the nearest river and floated down the waterways and into the mighty Daintree River. Here they were collected and shipped further south to eventually end up as decking and masts for the all-powerful British Navy and the trading ships of the East Indies Company.

The jungle landscape was slowly denuded with pockets of remnant forest left here and there across the valley.

The grass that took over the clearings was lush and green all year and so it wasn't long for enterprising dairy farmers to show interest.

The Johnsons were one such family and packed up their meagre belongings at Tyalgum in northern New South Wales and moved their brood to the Daintree.

∽o∾

Burton and Marion Johnson had five children under the age of ten when they arrived in Rockhampton.

When they left, they had six children and the latest arrival was Max.

Max was born on 4th June 1926 and within days had joined the rest of the family as they chugged along the Pacific Ocean coast in the ferry heading for the mouth of the dangerous Daintree River.

As the ferry wended its way up the river the family soon learned of the dangers that lurked in the shadows and murky depths. They were well warned by the time they reached the jetty that serviced the district.

The jetty was a wooden one and stood below a steep embankment. On the top of the hill was the mainstay of the area, a butter factory, and nearby a timber mill.

The family settled into life in the Daintree readily milking twice a day and clearing the rainforest sapping the energy of their father, Burton, and his oldest son, Burt. Once the farm was fully cleared and the dairy herd numbers at a maximum, life became more predictable and they had to seek out ways to entertain themselves.

Max and his older brother, Keith, soon became mates and got up to all sorts of mischief until a fateful day when they came across a huge crocodile wallowing in the billabong below the farmhouse.

Max had ended up the scapegoat when all along he was the only one who told the truth of what had happened.

His fate was almost worse than death as he was thoroughly thrashed by his father with a lawyer cane and then cut off by the family. He was called a liar and a blasphemer by his father and disowned by his mother. The ostracism cut deeper than the welts that bled from his backside.

In the meantime, life went on for the other eight siblings. The older girls Madeline, Isobel, and Eva were the work slaves for the dairy. They milked the numerous cows twice a week including weekends. Then they churned the milk and syphoned off the cream. The younger ones included the twins Rita and Phyllis along with Molly and the baby Marge continued to grow and add years to their birthdays.

Burt had become friendly with another teenager who lived in the valley. He was Andrew Hindmarsh or Andy as he preferred to be called. Burt and Andy got to wandering off into the nearby hills each carrying a 22 rifle that they had received as birthday presents when they turned 18.

As Andy got his rifle first Burt would tag along on the hunt and often be allowed to load and fire the gun at the animals that crossed their paths.

Wild piglets and the occasional rabbit were always a welcome addition to the family dinner table.

Keith and Max were somewhat jealous of their older sibling and his mate as they were able to wander so freely through the countryside.

The older boys often left home just after milking at 6.30 am and returned at 4.30 pm in time to round up the herd and drive them to the milking shed.

One beautiful spring morning twelve-year-old Keith plucked up the courage to follow Burt and Andy into the rainforest. He watched their every move until they reached the edge of the bush.

Keith marked the position in his mind where the two boys had stepped into the thick and foreboding rainforest. He waited for the count of 30 giving the hunters a half a minute head start. He ran from his hiding place to the position he had marked and found confusion. His brain began shouting different places and he gave up and turned to go home.

He stopped after several steps took a big breath turned and ran at the trees and creepers. His bravado pushed him a few yards in and he felt he was on the right track. He stepped and stopped doing this in several directions. All the time he was searching desperately for the tracking signs.

Nothing

At this time he panicked and began rushing around and screaming for help.

Luckily Burt and Andy had not gone too far and upon hearing the protestations of Burt's younger brother ran back to help him. "Sit down and stay still Keith or else you will work your way further into the bush and further away from us. Now count to ten and call 'help' so we can get a direction on your whereabouts."

They gave Keith a good dressing down about the danger of becoming lost and what might happen to him. They even added emphasis by retelling the story that their great-grandfather Ambrose had passed down through the family of the three little boys who became lost and perished in Daylesford, Victoria, way back in the 1860s.

Keith, with his tail between his legs, sulked home and vowed never to venture into the rainforest alone.

He heard his inner voice making the promise but in reality, was not entirely put off by the idea of following the older boys as they often came home with enticingly unbelievable stories.

Chapter 2

One of these fascinating stories, that Keith had over-heard, involved skinny dipping with the Thompson girls at the pool further up the Stewart Creek.

This was an isolated pool surrounded by thick remnant forest and very hard to penetrate. The boys had managed to slash their way in and enjoy the cooling water and the quiet.

One day they had mentioned their secret pool to Jess, the eldest of the Thompson girls. She immediately told her two sisters who were intrigued by the idea of having a secret little hideaway hardly 200 yards from their backyard.

Jess was sent back to Burt and Andy with the message that all three would like to meet them there to have a swim and some fun.

The rendezvous was arranged for the next day and it turned out to be the best time all five young people ever had. Jess and her two sisters, Annabel and Coral all went home in the happiest of moods.

These meetings continued for the rest of spring and then stopped because the wet season set in and it was too dangerous to venture near the creek.

Torrential monsoon rains caused massive flooding across the entire Daintree catchment area and was an annual event. It kept all the farming families trapped inside the home paddock and their houses.

Worse still were the flash floods that would come crashing along the valleys, sweeping all before them and giving little chance of survival to any living creature that happened to be caught by the raging torrent.

Keith had overheard the stories of the frolics at the pool in late February when the wet season was on the wane. He was determined to follow the older boys and watch the three girls cavorting in the pool in their one-piece swimsuits.

His interest in girls had taken hold over eight months ago at school when one of the Sweetman twins, Jennifer, had been told to hold his hand during the learning of a folk dance.

She was a pretty blond and he always thought she would make a girlfriend but he could never speak to her.

So, to touch her hand was special. The heat that flowed from her fingers into her palms and across to his hands was delicious and he felt his whole body reacting to the warmth.

As she pirouetted, he caught a scent of her powder, that she applied liberally across her chest every morning and he felt an overpowering desire. He tried desperately to keep control and to follow the dance step and the teacher's instructions.

As the music came to a stop, he realised he had a monster in his shorts. He looked desperately around to see if anyone else noticed his predicament. He had to get out of the crowd before someone pointed out the bulge in his shorts.

He babbled an excuse for the need to rush urgently to the toilet and luckily the teacher noted his contorted face and agreed.

Keith raced across the grass towards the dunny feeling the monster bouncing up and down, totally unrestrained. This movement only added to his woes and as he slammed the dunny door behind him he felt his first ever orgasm.

At first, it was a shock then a glow came over him and a feeling of tiredness so he slumped onto the seat, reached down, and took the stiff member in his hand. As he held on a delightful feeling swept across his whole body.

"What the hell happened?" he thought trying to recall the episode from beginning to end. Whatever it was had to do with Jenny and therefore it must be a girl thing.

He looked down and noticed that his penis had now gone flaccid and was back to normal.

He stood up and tried to have a pee. Surprisingly this was difficult and it took some time before a few dribbles appeared and then a jerking of a few streams.

Something had happened inside his penis that had caused it to become stiff, to give that wonderful feeling and to not be able to pee normally. To Keith, all these mysteries needed further investigation.

He soon found that he could do his work in getting the hard-ons and the orgasmic feelings.

He discussed these with Max to see if he was feeling the same way but the kid didn't seem to be interested or maybe he was too immature to have it happening.

Keith suggested Max pick Jenny Sweetman as a folk dance partner and see if the same thing happened to him. He gave Max a very vivid account of what had occurred suggesting the dancing hold would create the same emotions in the younger boy.

Max's report several days later left Keith deflated and confused. "Why did it only happen to him and not his young brother?" he pondered.

Keith was however smitten by this girl thing whatever it was and he planned to find out more. He had noticed that the older girls at school had boobies that kept growing.

He certainly noticed that Eva, his older sister had large breasts and he wondered what these might look like if there was no clothing between his eyes and the flesh. He began to search of ways to catch a glimpse of these new interests.

Nothing seemed to get him a look as the girls were always sure they locked the doors and pulled the curtains when undressing or dressing.

Keith tried asking Molly to describe her older sisters in the nude but she told him he was nuts and if his mother found out he was talking like that he would get a hiding. She explained that everyone had 'private parts' and that it was wrong to look at another person's 'bits and pieces' and he needed to put these ideas out of his mind.

If he settled down and waited until he was sixteen he would get the "Birds and Bees" talk and all he needed to know would be revealed. If he listened to his half-baked schoolmates or older siblings, they would more than likely get things all mixed up.

Molly's final advice to Keith was to keep all his questions to himself and whatever he decided to do never ask his parents or his teachers. They are old-fashioned and see the girl-boy activity as smutty or dirty.

Try as he might Keith just found the mystery grow and the hard-ons became impossible to control so when Keith heard about the secret swimming hole and the Thompson girls, he became hell-bent on finding it and watching what went on.

⚬

The only way he could follow the two older boys was if he had a partner in crime and the only one to fit that description was little brother, Max.

Keith approached Max with a different ploy suggesting that they follow the older boys so they could learn tracking skills in the rainforest. These skills he suggested would help them become trackers for the police in later life, a very worthy career.

Max had become circumspect about life after his thrashing and spent most of his hours inside his head living out fantasies.

He also became fascinated by the local indigenous people and would sit for hours above their makeshift camps observing them. The tribe visited once a year on their walkabout. They built their mia-mias well away from the billabong so that if any crocodiles were living in the creek, they would get warned in time to take evasive action.

The chief of the tribe was King Billy and he was a friend of Burton. Annually they would meet to talk about the hunting and to exchange food for aboriginal artifacts.

The tribe would be seen from the kitchen window arriving with the women and children together carrying the tribal belongings and foodstuff. The women would be first and selected the place where the camp would be set-up. Two of the warriors would break away from the other men and search the entire area looking for signs of danger.

The most potent danger in the Daintree River valley was the huge crocodiles. They lived on the river banks in packs where the bull was the boss and he had several females. The tell-tale signs of crocodile activity were large footprints and next was the dragging of the long armoured tail.

The adolescent females carrying babies and implements to make meals kept together and ran an eye over their little ones to ensure they were kept safe.

The warriors and old men held the rear and had their weapons in readiness to run down and kill any source of food.

Chapter 3

Keith was mesmerised by the tracking skills of the older warriors and one day he asked Max to go with him and talk to the aboriginal warriors. The boys approached them asking how they could see tracks made by animals and birds. Keith and Max could not see any nor could they read the story that the tracks left behind.

The old men had several young fellows with them and suggested that Max might like to join in the day's hunting and get to learn the bushcraft that the youths were being tutored in.

Max and Keith keenly accepted the invitation. To the pleasure and amazement of the elders, Max proved to be a quick learner and one with patience and persistence. Keith tried hard but had little patience and tended to walk over the tracks and thereby rub them out. Max determined that whenever he got the opportunity to join the tribe as it passed through his father's farm he would take the invitation to join the hunting parties.

Slowly he became a clever tracker.

He learnt to observe the tracks of different birds and animals as they moved about the undergrowth or along the muddy creek banks. He became adept at determining the time the tracks were made and what activity had occurred.

He especially enjoyed listening to the sounds of the rainforest and could tell and mimic many of the hundreds of birds that inhabited the Daintree Valley.

He learned how to shimmy up the tallest of trees to collect eggs, honey, or orchids. The latter were sold to the wives of the local farmers as beautiful flower displays on their verandahs.

At home, he would follow his sisters to and from the barn watching their footfalls and determining what was happening to the grass and the soft soil beneath. It wasn't long before he could tell who was moving by and whether they were walking, running, and even what mood they were in.

When Max was asked by Keith to follow the bigger boys into the rainforest, he didn't hesitate.

As much as he found Keith a boorish prig, he couldn't push aside the opportunity to improve his tracking and bush skills and show up his older brother. It even allowed him to lose the nasty piece of work deep in the forest as revenge for all the hurt he had caused. "Revenge in any form would be delicious to behold," he thought to himself.

Burt and Andy called their goodbyes soon after breakfast on an overcast day and with rifles slung over their shoulders set out for the rainforest at the back of the block.

Keith immediately yelled to Max that he was going to the bog for a pee and set off. Max raced after him pretending to hold on to himself looking like he was next in line.

Keith entered the dunny and closed the door while Max went past and hid behind the toilet. Keith came out hitching up his shorts and wandered to where Max was hiding.

A glance told them no one was watching so they took off hell for leather to the chook shed then along the fence of the pigsty and into the orchard. They nestled into the hanging branches of the fig tree.

After carefully looking all round and deciding all was clear they bent low and ran for the tree line. Max raced into the bush but stopped a few yards in. He began searching around until he came upon the clear imprint of a boot.

"This is where they went in, now we can follow them, let's go," he said to Keith.

Keith took his hat off, scratched his head and said, "How the hell can you see anything on the ground it looks like a wet soppy mess of dead leaves and mud to me?"

"Never mind, come on they've got a good start on us we need to move fast." Max led, looking for the tell-tale signs that showed the two older boys had made their way into this part of the forest.

A broken twig, a slip on the wet leaves, hand mark on a tree trunk to keep upright, a piece of material that had been caught on one of the stay-a-while plants. All these little signs enabled Max to keep on their trail.

Keith was trying to keep up but was nowhere near as sure footed or confident as his nine-year-old brother. He was about to start protesting about being lost and that Max had no idea where he was going when they pulled up short to the sound of a young girl squealing in delight.

"They're just ahead. Go quietly and keep low. If we get seen we are dead meat," said Max.

Another fifty yards and they came upon the bank of the creek. It arose abruptly above the flood plain and huge boulders were scattered here and there. The two youngsters raised their heads a little above the bank and looked twenty yards down towards the cool waters of the pool that the five swimmers were frolicking in.

∽o∽

Keith gave a gasp when he saw that the three girls were in one piece bathing costumes. That whet his sexual appetite and he felt his member start to stiffen. He reached down and touched it willing it to stay calm for a little while.

Premature ejaculation was the enemy of every man and once spent they lose that fierce and delightful desire. "Hang in there, old fellow," he whispered.

Max looked at his older brother and scratched his head. Who the heck was Keith talking to and what did he mean by 'hang in there old fellow?' He decided not to get into a discussion and kept quiet.

He was scouting the area ahead and selected the far end where several large boulders had been washed down in a flood. These he felt would provide the cover for their clandestine mission.

Max got Keith's attention and jabbed a finger in the direction of the boulders and without waiting for a reply slid back down the bank and ran doubled over towards the boulders. Keith reluctantly followed.

The three boulders were perfectly situated as two were close together allowing them to look across the pool.

Anyone looking their way would barely see them as the gap was only half a foot wide. The third smaller boulder was a yard away and protecting their bodies from onlookers so that they could sit up and watch the fun going on in the pool.

∞

Most of the frolicking was in good taste with little sexual interactions, much to Keith's disappointment.

Every now and again one of the boys would lift a girl high above his head and throw her into the water. Gales of laughter then spluttering would follow.

Keith thought they were too far from the action and that he would miss any of the female anatomy that might peek out from a loosening swimsuit but Max was steadfast.

"We stay here, there's no way they can see us."

∞

After what appeared to have been an hour by the angle of the sun all the swimmers retired to the beach on the same side as the youngsters' hideout.

Keith was annoyed as this meant only one of the girls could be seen and she was lying on her towel on her side facing away from them. He was impressed by the way the swimsuit material was riding into the slit of her bottom so that kept him interested.

Chapter 4

Suddenly they ducked as footsteps were heard close by and coming towards them. One of the Thompson girls was making for the very place that they were hiding. She appeared around the first rock and stood looking back at the group.

She called sheepishly, "No peeking you lot I need to pee."

Keith was shocked but delighted with this declaration while Max tried desperately to make himself as tiny as possible.

Andy called out. "Why don't you walk into the water up to your waist and do it that way?"

The girl answered and she sounded very close. "I'm here now so leave me to concentrate."

The young lady was oblivious to the two youngsters who cowered no less than a yard away. All she had to do was look between the space of the two rocks and their game would have been up. They would have got a nice old beating from the two older boys.

"Hurry up Tracey," called one of the other girls, "I'm going next. You've started a stampede and found the ideal spot all in one. I can't hold on for much longer."

Keith's heart skipped a beat and he strained to see the girl who was so close yet untouchable. He had a name, Tracey, and that made the fantasy even more exciting. Max dared not breathe.

Tracy unhooked her swimsuit strap from her right shoulder and as it fell her nakedness was partly exposed. Keith lost all control. He was delirious with the body that was slowly being exposed in front of him but angry because his fun was over so quickly.

Max couldn't believe what was happening. He had never seen nor was interested in girls before but what he was looking at, caused a surge of desire and he felt parts of his body stiffening and tingling.

Tracey slid the strap over her elbow and flicked it off her wrist. She proceeded to do the same with the left strap of the swimsuit. She now was crouching forward towards the two boys. They could see her in her all togetherness and she innocently went about her business.

Tracy struggled to push the wet swimsuit below her waist and then down past her knees. The young girl pushed her legs astride and moved onto her haunches. Max heard the slow drip, drip, and then a stream of urine. After some time, the drips came back and then Tracey stood up and pulled the swimsuit back into its correct position. Keith was deflated.

Everything seemed to happen too fast and he wanted a replay.

Max was still in shock and then he got a whiff of a smell that would stay with him forever. Urine has a distinct smell for all different animals and he could smell the unique smell of human piss. There was a distinctive odour of ammonia. It wafted past fleetingly.

Max was ecstatic as he had fixed another arrow to his tracking bow. Unknowingly this singular experience would save many lives in the future.

Tracey was walking away and calling out, "Sis try somewhere else I think I flooded this area and the smell isn't too nice."

"Damn," thought Keith, "I thought we were going to get another one to look at." Keith felt a fierce tug on his shirt collar and realised Max was ready to take off. He couldn't afford to be left in the forest by himself so reluctantly he rolled away, jumped into a crouch, and raced after the fast-vanishing silhouette of his baby brother. They made it home in good time and the older boys had no notion that they had seen them frolicking with the girls in the billabong

Max's world was one of trial and tribulation as he grew stronger and smarter in the most dangerous environment on the Australian continent. His love of the outdoors and his father's guilt allowing him to wander free gave him a magical upbringing. However, all good things soon ceased and new tragedies and adventures took hold.

His oldest sister Madeline was a sickly child with a liver complaint. She had fallen in love with a boy from the nearby town of Atherton. The two married and shifted out of the Daintree.

A few months after the marriage Maddy was delighted to tell her mother that she was pregnant. Marion couldn't wait to tell Burton and the family. She was even more excited to tell the district folk that she was going to be a grandmother.

All the while that she spread the good tidings surrounding the pregnancy Marion had a dread of what this might mean for her daughter. She had protected and made life as easy as possible for her child. She often revisited the the doctor's prophesy back in Tyalgum when Maddy was barely four years old, "Your daughter has troubles with her liver and will need special treatment off and on across her early years. When she reaches adulthood, her health will deteriorate and she will become bedridden. There is little I can do. You and your family need to give her a happy life."

The family obliged on the pretext that Maddy was the family's special child. Marion and Burton did not disclose the reason they gave Maddy the adoration of "Our special girl" when she was having a turn or being rushed to the hospital.

The pregnancy and the disastrous combination resulted in the loss of mother and child.

The whole family was devastated. For such a young life to be lost is sad enough but two at the same time was unbearable.

After the death of his eldest sister, Madeline, Max found himself on the back of the model T ford headed out of the Daintree. There had been much soul searching and countless whispered meetings between his mother and father then suddenly they were all packed and going.

As his father Burton said, "The demons have found us we have to leave."

The family wandered the north of Queensland picking up farm work wherever it was available. They tried to avoid the back-breaking sugarcane harvesting. Lighting the fires to clear out the undergrowth and the snakes was fun.

On the other hand, it was not much fun slashing away to cut down a dozen six-foot lengths of canes with a machete while on the lookout for a deadly taipan or two.

Once you had the bundle tightly held you ran the machete along the sides of each cane to expose the woody part. These canes were then loaded on the midget-sized steam trains. The train tracks went in every direction through the cane-growing area.

Most of the time the family camped on dairy farms, helping with the milking, separating, and delivering the cream to the butter factories.

In September 1939 the World once more spiralled into pandemonium. The Germans, under their madman leader, Hitler, sent troops into Poland starting the Second World War. Most people shrugged their shoulders and continued their routines expecting the major powers to deal forthrightly with the madman. It was not to be and when stormtroopers rushed into the Lowlands and captured Belgium on May 10, 1940 countries of the World looked up and pondered. A monster had been unleashed and through the appeasement policies that had been thrown around by Britain and France, Germany believed it had the strength and technology to take over the World.

The German blitzkrieg set in motion a mobilisation of young men throughout the British Empire. Australian youngsters began arriving at recruiting stations in their hundreds ready to take on the Hun and have the business over and done in days.

Australia, as a member of the British Empire, was dragged into the conflict. Young men from all walks of life and places walked to recruiting stations to sign up.

Some under the age jacked up their ages to be part of the adventure. All the talk was of how quickly the mighty British Empire would wipe the grin off the Krauts' faces and settle Europe back to peace.

∽∽

The Johnson boys were all kept well away from the recruiters and those who were signing up. They continued to work away at their jobs almost oblivious to the overseas situation. This all changed in December 1941, when the Japanese attacked Pearl Harbour,

Hawaii where the Americans had their 5th Fleet sitting at anchor.

The raid was a major victory for Japan as the unsuspecting Yanks were savagely mauled by wave after wave of fighter planes. Hawaii was left a burning wreck with thousands killed. Japan was on the march sweeping south through China, Southeast Asia, the Philippines, and Indonesia and at the same time moving their superior fleets into the Pacific Ocean.

One morning the Johnson family was eating breakfast when news on the radio herald the fall of the impenetrable fortress at Singapore. Thousands of Australian soldiers along with their allies were trapped and either killed or taken prisoner.

"The way the Japs are moving Australia will be attacked soon," mused Keith as he stuffed a piece of toast spread with vegemite into his mouth. "We all need to be willing to defend what is ours and we need to do it offshore to the north. If we wait for the bastards to get onto the mainland we are done for."

Burton frowned but nodded sagely before commenting. "You are right my boy but war is bloody and brutal so think wisely before rushing into a decision."

"All I can think about is all those poor buggers who are interned in places like Changi and Hellfire Pass and those doing it tough in the jungles of New

Guinea. We all have to help out or the country is doomed."

∽o∽

Max who was 15 years old sat staring at his father and older sibling playing the scenes in his mind. Soldiers rushed across shallow creeks firing their heavy 303s at a hidden enemy while from machine gun nests came the steady and deadly rat-a-tat-tat of enemy fire. Men with their slouch hats clinging to their heads tied down under their chins with leather binding spun and danced as bullets slammed into their bodies. Some died instantly and lay floating in the ever growing red of the water, while others writhed in agony screaming for help as their life ebbed from them.

"Max you alright?" The question jolted Max from his dreaming and he looked across at his father.

"I must join up as soon as I can, I need to be there for my Aussie mates and to keep mum and the girls safe and free."

"That can't and won't happen under my watch son. You are barely 15 years old and the recruitment officer will reject you point blank. Any way in three years' time when you are of age the whole mess will be sorted and we should be living a normal happy life. You mark my words."

∽o∽

Keith contemplated joining the army, mostly because his mates had rushed off to the recruitment office and signed. Every time Keith met up with one of these fellows, they were full of tales of fun, frolic and camaraderie. During the chats the soldier boys would go on and on about the uniform and how it was so attracting to women. Apparently, they could not walk down a street without a female on both arms.

Keith was fed up with being dad's little slave on the dairy farm and could see no way out. The old man was driven by a work ethic that was almost crippling to youngsters like Max and the girls. Keith wanted an out and the Army seemed the opportunity he had been searching for.

Chapter 5

Burt was the eldest and was concerned for his future especially as he was building a large and profitable business. He went to discuss the dilemma he had with his father.

"Why don't you offer to be a private transport company for the army. They will be searching for ways to move troops and equipment without having to train drivers and make new trucks. If they agreed then you would get an exemption from military action and make a fortune from the venture."

Burt had nothing to lose so he brought a ticket on the train from Brisbane to Sydney in August, 1940. He found a recruiting station clearly signed by a poster with an officer standing pointing directly into the eyes of each passer-by and seeming to shout at them, "Your country needs you".

He joined the line-up which stretched back a block and waited patiently, shuffling forward as each new recruit emerged excitedly brandishing his papers.

He finally made it to the steps and into the building. It was a squat office with a bare table on which sat a large ink blotter and an ink well from which protruded three pens. There were two wire filing trays one to the left said IN the other to the right OUT.

Behind the desk, dressed in khaki uniform sat a soldier. He didn't bare any stripes so Burt took him for a private. He sat to attention and dealt with each young man with a loud voice and few words. "Name, birthday, address, next of kin, permission to join, sign here, you're in, report to the station at 1200 hours today."

Burt stood in front of the little private and asked to speak to the commanding officer about an offer of transport for the army.

The request and the confidence in Burt's voice threw the young private as he was trained to only go through one process and he had that fixed firmly in his head. Any deviation from the script would cause a meltdown. He had never received a request like this. He ummed and erred and finally went to a desk at the back of the room.

There was a lot of whispering and pointing and finally a big potbellied sergeant pushed his considerable weight out of the chair and wandered across to Burt.

"Transport eh, might be of some use, come through and tell me a bit more."

Burt put his case and the sergeant warmed to the possibility of a civvy running troops and machinery up and down the east coast especially considering the distances from Melbourne to Port

Douglas. "As long as you supply the drivers and the petrol, we'll pay you piecemeal for each run. You'd better be efficient and punctual at all times. There will be some missions that cannot be discussed with anyone so discretion will be paramount. Have we got a deal?"

Burt was elated now he had the contract in his hand it should be easy peasy to talk his two brothers into joining him and they will all make it alive through this damn war. He jumped and clicked his heals as he headed for the railway station.

Max had waited at the gate of the Tully Army Training Centre for his older brother Keith to appear then they would catch the bus home to Kenmore. He had hitched his way north from Brisbane over the past two days hoping he could catch up with big brother and join him on his furlough.

Once at the gate the sergeant on guard wouldn't let him inside nor would he alert Keith as to his presence. That left Max patiently sitting under a tree on the far side of the road admiring the huge sign in yellow lettering on a black background, "Tully Australian Infantry Forces Jungle Warfare Training Centre."

The wait grew longer and Max became restless so he wandered up the road to an intersection and from here he could look down upon the little town of Tully. The dominant feature was the Sugar Cane Refinery that belched steam and smoke into the grey sky. On his way to the town it was the smoke that had first indicated he was nearing his destination. It could be seen for miles and miles around.

As he admired the sugarcane fields that abound in all directions two youths came flat out towards him on a motorbike.

Max loved anything mechanical so the bike caught his eye and he was suitably impressed and became even more so when he realised it was a Triumph Tiger 100. It gleamed in the sunlight and was in stark contrast to the rider and his pillion passenger. Both were young, wiry and dressed in dirty black overalls and wore black singlets.

The bike was laid down low and came on sideways towards Max. He jumped to one side to avoid being hit and was ready to give a fair bit of lip when the rider miraculously regained the balance, hauled the bike to a standing position and stopped it in the centre of the intersection.

"Want to buy a bike mister?" asked the pillion passenger as he jumped off backwards and sauntered to Max.

Max was taken aback by the casual question and the confidence shown by what looked like a 14-year-old kid. "What's it worth?" he asked.

"For you an easy £200 but we are giving out bargains cause our big brother has been called up and has to flog it off fast. Let's say an even £125."

Max couldn't contain himself and without thinking reached for his wallet, peeled off the £125 and handed it over. "Done deal old son it's all yours, best bike they ever made was the Triumph Tiger 100."

He swapped places with the rider and balanced the bike getting a feel for it and revving the engine to catch the power in the motor.

The two would be salesmen had scampered, slapping each other on the back as they ran. Max eased in the first gear and the bike shot forward. He added acceleration and changed to second gear. The bike rode smooth and it didn't take long to reach the army barracks gates. He past the gates did a long sweeping U turn and stopped on the side opposite the barracks.

Max revved the engine and turned off the key. He set the bike on its wheel stand, climbed off and sat back under the tree. He had something to brag about to Keith and a set of wheels to take them both home.

Now he had his freedom, the freedom he had always yearned. He could go anywhere with the wind blowing through his jet black, wavy hair, a smile on his face and a carefree attitude. He could pick up the chicks as he sped from town to town selecting them at will as they all loved to feel the throbbing of a motorbike between their thighs.

❧

It was nearly 1800 hours before Keith appeared in his khaki uniform and a brown duffel Johnson bag swung over one shoulder

"Smarten up got to get a snap for your folk before the Japs cut off that mug from the rest of you." It was Thommo, one of Keith's best mates from his barracks. Keith looked up and realised what Thommo was talking about. Then on the side of the road he saw brother Max sitting on a motorcycle.

Max chugged the bike towards him passed through the gate and stopped a few feet away. The brothers embraced and Max said, "Don't ask?"

He pointed to Keith, beckoning him to climb onto the pillion seat.

Thommo held a Brownie that he was shading with one hand and searching for the trigger with the other. Max grabbed Keith's slouch hat, turned it upside down on his head then turned side on to get his face in the shot.

"Smile for the birdy," chirped Thommo and about six other soldiers, all dressed in khaki whom had stopped to admire the motorbike, all mimicked the request with a few added expletives.

❧

"You've got three days furlough Keith you lucky sod so make the most of it. Say hello to those gorgeous twin sisters of yours and plant a kiss on their lips. You never know what might be happening to us all by the time you get back.

Keith noted a tear form in Thommo's right eye but he ignored it. Max revved up the engine, flicked in the clutch, released the brake lever and accelerated towards the main gate of the compound.

A sergeant with MP attached around his upper left biceps held up an arm to signal the bike rider to stop. The bike pulled up and the Sergeant indicated a cut across the throat with his hand and Max turned off the engine and gave a silly salute.

The Triumph Tiger 100 gurgled to a stop. Keith moved forward ready to mount the motorbike behind Max.

"Name and rank soldier," bawled the Sergeant.

"Oh, come on sarge for Chrissake you know who I am. Do we have to play silly games just let me go so I can get home? It's over a hundred miles down the track," said Keith.

"Name, rank and papers and that's the last order I repeat or you'll spent the night in the slammer instead of trying to run a hand or two up some floozy's dress."

Keith knew he was wasting his own time so he yelled back, "Private Johnson, QX60198, 13/33rd battalion, sir," he saluted with the long way around shortest way down method that had been drilled into him and his mates over the last five months.

He handed a sheet of paper to the sergeant who glanced at it and said, "Lucky man. This may be your last rest for a while enjoy it. Don't be late on Thursday at 1700 hours that's when your leave finishes.

Keith felt a shudder racing up his back and the hairs on the nape of his neck crawled. There was something in the tone of the Sergeant's voice that made him feel that something big was going down and he and his mates were to get their first taste of action.

The sergeant saluted, raised the barrier and Max accelerated the heavy bike out onto the main road.

∞

He turned east where in a few minutes he met up with the main street of Tully.

He turned onto the road and idled through the little town. He felt terribly important as he drove sedately down the hill towards the river with Keith clinging on to his back. The town had shops on either side and people were busily going about closing their shops. Several raised their hands and waved to the young soldier on the motorbike.

They didn't know him but the boy brought back memories of their days either in the army or riding a motorbike.

They reached the main highway and turned south. The road ran along the east coast all the way from Sydney to Cairns. It was bituminised although barely one lane wide.

Max switched on the headlights as the gloom of the evening was quickly turning to darkness.

Chapter 6

The number of army trucks and other motorised vehicles using the road had cut it up badly so Max had to keep his speed down. It was a long ride with several toilet breaks before they found the turn off to Kenmore just outside of the sprawling city of Brisbane.

It was up in the hills that their family had a dairy farm and this was their destination. The dirt road soon disappeared and it was lucky they knew their way around as it was poorly signposted.

With little traffic to contend with and a nice deep furrow to follow, Max gunned the bike and watched as the speedometer needle edged towards 60 mph. It was exhilarating and he felt that freedom coursing through his veins. He did a light backhander into Keith's ribs who acknowledged with a pat on the shoulder.

Mile after mile was gobbled up until they topped a rise and pulled up. To one side there was a pretty white washed wooden chapel with a red corrugated iron roof. This was where the Johnsons went to church. Max was past believing in any Gods as his life experiences had killed off any such beliefs.

Way down in the valley the boys could barely make out a farm house with a wisp of white smoke rising lazily from a stone chimney. Their mother was expecting them and she would be slaving over the stove making a pork stew and baking scones. The scones would be spread with home-made strawberry jam and smothered with boiled cream.

Max felt his mouth salivate and he pushed the bike forward, felt the balance and accelerated towards home and his family.

His mother and sisters all came running out of the house as soon as they caught the first sound from the motorbike. They had not expected anyone to arrive riding a beautiful shiny bike and never in their wildest dreams did they think it would be their little brother Max with big brother Keith riding pillion behind.

They were covered with kisses from Molly and Marge and then lined up the twins to offer Thommo's kisses on the lips. There was much spitting and wiping of the droplets of saliva when Rita and Phyllis were told who had sent the kisses. Ma Johnson, Marion, embraced Keith into her ample bosom and started weeping.

Keith tried to explain that he was home for three days so she should be happy not sad. He also managed to gasp out that if she kept squeezing him like she was he would probably die from lack of oxygen within the next few minutes.

Max unclipped the swag from the pillion passenger seat and arm in arm with Marion on one side and Keith on the other they walked into the kitchen.

As they predicted, there was a pork stew bubbling on the wood fire and a dozen scones with strawberry jam and cream in the centre of the table. Everyone sat down and the questions flew in all directions. "Whoa," said Max and he held up a hand. "One at a time or we'll never follow what you are saying. Eldest first, so what's on your mind mum?"

Marion wiped a tear from her eye and muttered something about the steam from the stew getting in her eye and said, "How far into New Guinea are the Japs and does that mean you will be fighting soon?"

Keith picked up half a scone and shovelled it all into his mouth. He chewed a few times and swallowed. "Not sure to both questions, ma," he said trying to remain vague as he knew they were all as frightened as he and his mates were.

The Japanese were one of the finest trained armies in the World and terribly aggressive. Some of the horrific stories that were emerging from battle hardened troops returning from south east Asia and the Pacific region had left little doubt that the Japanese were hell bent on taking over Australia and that they had no intention of keeping captives unless they were able to carry out strong labouring jobs. Women and sick men had been put to the sword or machine gunned.

Keith had had this drilled into his head daily and had formed the opinion that he would rather die than be captured. However, he kept all this to himself as he didn't want the family to feel defeated nor concerned for his safety, and that of his other soldiers related to the family.

"We are being trained in the latest warfare with the best equipment so we should be able to turn things around. Our jungle warfare training at Tully is being replicated all along the Queensland coast so by the time they need reinforcements we will be fully trained." Keith said all this with more conviction than he felt but everyone in the kitchen seemed to relax.

"Have you got a girlfriend yet?" asked Marge the youngest.

"You're out of turn bubs, you're the youngest. No I haven't got a girl but I have danced with plenty. We have a dance every Saturday with the nurses from the Field Ambulance group."

The scones had disappeared when there was a commotion out the back and Max and Keith recognised his father's voice. Keith felt a hotness flush over him as he waited for the old man to enter the room.

"Well, well what has the cat dragged in here," said Burton as he made his way across to Keith. The two embraced and Burton slapped his son on the back.

"I'm real proud of you Keith and your brother Burt, for serving your country."

Keith was searching his father's face and demeanour to ascertain if there was any sarcasm or insincerity and he was shocked to find neither. The last time they had spoken was when Keith asked his father to sign his papers to join the army. Burton had poo pooed the idea telling the boy he was too young and too gutless.

Keith was taken back but persisted with his desire to join and serve his country. In the end the old fellow snatched the paper from Keith and scribbled his signature and date.

Keith took the paper and without a word he left vowing never to return. His promise didn't last too long as on the third day of moving into the Tully Army Barracks he became revoltingly homesick and cried himself to sleep each night. The camp doctor dispensed some strong sleeping tablets and within a week he had ceased pining for his mother and sisters. He couldn't have cared about his father.

For now he was content to be in the arms of his loving family and the warmth of the kitchen.

⧫

The three days vanished rapidly and even though plenty was spoken about and questions answered, Keith was soon ready to return to the Tully Army Barracks.

Keith borrowed the motorcycle from Max and was soon gunning the Triumph Tiger 100 up the mountainside and away from the valley. As the ground flattened out he turned the accelerator and watched the speedometer needle climb steadily to 70mph. He thrilled at the cold air rushing through his hair and chilling his chest.

He was welcomed into barracks at Tully by a salute from the sergeant who had seen him off three days ago. "You need to ditch that heap of shit and get to the parade ground. The Colonel will be addressing everyone within the next five minutes. If you're late I'll personally kick you up the arse."

Keith returned a quick, "Yes sir." He parked the Triumph Tiger 100 near his barracks, threw the swag through the double doors and ran flat out for the parade ground.

He shuffled into position between Thommo and another bloke he'd never seen before just as the Parade Sergant Major bawled out, "Attention!"

∽०∽

Again there was a lot of shuffling and in it all Thommo whispered, "You sure know how to cut things fine. Do I get my kisses now or later?"

Colonel Blight stepped forward and acknowledged the Parade Sergeant's introduction with a nod. He stopped at the edge of a wooden dais that placed him a foot above the parade ground. It wouldn't have mattered as he was tall and slender standing well over six and a half foot. He was in full military uniform with brass pieces catching the afternoon sun. A row of multi-coloured medals stood importantly on the left side of his chest. He was wearing an officer's cap that was tilted slightly to his right. He had a voice that was like a fog horn.

"Men of the Australian Fighting Forces you will be taking up the fight against the scourge of the Japanese forthwith."

All the while that this booming voice echoed over the parade ground and off into the nearby hills Keith was being torn between being scared out of his wits to being the hero who would deal with these slanty eyed invaders.

"Over the next fortnight you will be put through the most gruelling training you have ever faced. You need to be battle hardened and trained for jungle warfare. In two weeks, you will be fully armed and sent overseas to a destination yet to be selected. This will be a fight we must win or else the country you call Australia will capitulate to the Japanese and we will lose our hard-fought freedom forever. Train hard and train strong."

He stopped and saluted the parade who as one saluted back.

The parade sergeant called, "Dismissed."

"Well," thought Keith, "It looks like it will be on shortly. Lucky, I got my three days in before the announcement. I would assume that all future leave will be denied."

∽o∽

Keith marched off and headed for his barracks, As he was doing this his father and mother and the Johnson girls were settling into their new dairy farm. Burton had finally surrendered to the incessant request of his girls to move to the city. Brisbane was still a back water and seemed to be like that for the foreseeable future. The other Australian state capitals were beginning to catch up to the sky scraper architecture.

Burton had made a few enquiries and was offered a manager job on a dairy farm at Moggill Road, Kenmore, Brisbane.

The location proved to be a paradise for each of the Johnsons and for differing reasons.

To Marion it was her God's gift to her as it had a beautiful wooden chapel high on a nearby hill. Every opportunity she got she would walk from the farm along the muddy or dusty track called Moggill Road before steeling herself for the steep climb to the top.

Whoever selected the site for this chapel was trying to reach out to the hand of their God as it was the closest manmade object to Heaven for miles around. Mount Coo-tha was far in the distance towards the growing city of Brisbane but that was thought more of as the final resting place before the spirit left the body and ascended into the arms of the benevolent God. To the west were the mountains of the Great Dividing Range marching all the way from the far south of Victoria to Cape York.

Marion would contemplate all these and many more things Christian as she struggled to the top of the hill and then the final five steps up into the chapel. The exertion was all part of her penance and she relished reaching the chapel knowing that inside it would be cool and quiet where she could whisper her prayers and ask for the forgiveness of her sins since her last visit.

Often the children would accompany her but she didn't make it compulsory except for Sunday as there was so much to do on the dairy farm and her husband Burton was always insistent that work came first.

The older girls Isobel and Eva found that the other farms nearby were run by young gentleman. These fellows enjoyed the company of the girls and going to the dances that were held each Saturday was a must. The girls were treated like royalty as they were the first young ladies to set up permanently at Kenmore.

Each had no end of suitors calling in and asking them out.

The younger girls Molly, Phyllis and Rita were given more responsibility and when Burton arrived home one day driving a van they got a real boost in self-importance.

"Right ladies you are about to become the official milk vendors for the Johnson Dairy. You will learn to drive the van then become the milk deliverers. One to drive the other two cover left and right sides of the road while they deliver the milk and collect the money.

The game was on as each tried to outdo the other in getting their driver's licences.

Chapter 7

Queensland is in the tropics and it is hit every year where torrential rainfall and cyclones are characteristic of this type of climate. Life for the Johnson family shuddered to a halt one evening in 1942 when Keith arrived for tea. He announced he was joining up to do his bit for King and country. He had always been mentioned as the odd one out of the three boys even though he looked like his older brother Burt.

It was Max who should have been the odd one out as he was dark and swarthy like the Stewart side of the family. The other two boys bore the Danish ancestry, tall, fair skinned and reddish, straight hair.

At first Keith's father was silent and had shoved his meal away from himself. He seemed to be brooding, ready to explode. The family quietly waited for the full force of their father's acerbic tongue.

To the family's relief Burton picked up his fork, retrieved his plate and began picking at his food. Keith's demeanour relaxed and the girls all started to chatter about the day's activities.

Slowly the atmosphere in the room relaxed and then Burton said, "Your uncles did their bit and we won the First World War against those infuriating sanctimonious Jerries. If it wasn't for their willingness to stand up things may not have turned out for the better. Congratulations son and may God stay by your side."

Burton did not believe in God as he had seen too many people hurt and he reckoned that if there was this all-forgiving God who could perform miracles like curing the blind, walk on water, feed hundreds with a few fish and loaves and even bring children back from the dead then he should be doing this all the time. Where was this God Almighty when his darling daughter, Madeline was dying at the Atherton Hospital in 1936? He was nowhere to be seen when his precious young brother Keith had died from septicaemia after scratching a pimple back in 1913 and he was nowhere around when Reuben lost his face and his life in France and he didn't lift a finger to stop the Jerries from start-ing World War One and now where the hell is he when the World is on the brink of all-out war once again?

Having all those thoughts were one thing but he kept them to himself and his mates because he knew that Marion was a Believer, a strong Believer and she was not to be tangled with when it came to her unswerving belief in God and the Bible.

"You take care my boy," said Marion. "I want you back in one piece ."

The twins, Rita and Phyllis got up from the table and went around to Keith to give him a cuddle. Keith in his usual practical joking way ran in the opposite direction and into the lounge room.

Molly and then the youngest, Marge, joined in and the six-foot soldier lifted them all off the floor and swung them around in a slow circle before unceremoniously dumping them on the lounge chair.

He picked out Marge and began to tickle her vigorously. Her bubbly laughter filled the house and the other girls joined in the fun trying to tickle Keith. Shortly later the entire group lay exhausted. Marion got up from the table and began clearing away the dirty dishes and putting them in the hand basin that stood in for a sink.

Chapter 8

Max went to help and when he saw tears in his mother's eyes he cuddled into her breasts and said, "Don't worry mum I'm still here to look after you.

Anyway, Keithy will be alright because as you constantly remind us, 'God only takes the best and he takes them young' so I'd say Keith will outlive the lot of us."

Marion shushed him but a smile broke across her face. It was the first time that Max had noticed his mother had wrinkles and wondered if it was old age or all the stress of living in such dangerous and unknown times.

Next morning the farm was alive early with milking to be completed before the sun rose above the eastern horizon. Keith had come out on the verandah in a pair of boxer shorts and carrying two pair of boxing gloves. This was his favourite sport and Max was his favourite victim.

"I've invited a few mates up from the barracks for the day so hope you all don't mind," said Keith rather nonchantly. "You girls should be well pleased they're bonzer blokes and anyone of you might get a catch out of one of them."

"Yes, I could do with a husband who's about to go and get his head blown off. Me pregnant and him dead sounds a great way to enjoy the future," said Molly who always spoke her mind and was forthright.

"Come on Mol it's not like that we're all in the Infantry Corps so we don't go fighting. Some of us are non combatant like the medics and signals."

"Nah you just fix up the wounded, cut off shattered limbs and bury the ones that don't make it. Sounds like fun to me."

"Enough you two. It's fine Keith to invite your mates. In the meantime, let's see if Maxy boy has learnt that left jab, uppercut move we've been trying to teach him or will it be another out for 10 counts?" ventured Burton walking onto the verandah.

Max knew what was coming so he pulled off his shirt and took the black leather boxing gloves from his brother who towered over him some four inches.

Keith also had a reach advantage, three stone heavier and there were three years difference in age. He knew he would cop a fair bit of punishment before the old man called a stop or mum plead for mercy on his behalf.

Max pulled on the right-hand glove and his father tugged it in tight before turning the laces around and around his wrist. He then tied a bow before proceeding to do the same with the left glove.

Rita was busy helping Keith. She thought it was unfair that only the boys got to fight. She believed the girls could mix it just as well if they were given the skills and the knowledge.

She had always been the tomboy with Phyllis more refined and delicate. When it came to jobs around the farm, they were equally adept at the milking and separating.

When it came to delivering the milk to the locals and the townspeople it was Rita who did all the leg work. She even added more leg work when the twins saw a boy or drove passed the army barrack that was on the other side of town.

Phyllis on the other hand was happiest sitting in the driver's seat of the runner-about and steering the car from one gate to the next. She could barely see over the steering wheel but managed to get the job done and to get her sister and herself home safely each night.

Rita would stand on the running board holding a pail by the wire handle, ready to bound off through the next gate.

Here she would find another billy can with a lid and a wet piece of hessian hanging over it. She would remove the hessian and the lid before pouring the milk she had in her pail into the empty can. She then replaced the lid and hessian. She then scooped up the silver and bronze coins left nearby and scamper for the car.

Phyllis marvelled at her smooth operation and the fact that she never saw a drop of milk spilt or a sixpence left behind. As soon as Phyllis felt the thump of Rita landing on the running board, a she would let out the clutch and accelerate to the next house.

As the car chugged along Rita would take up a metal scoop with a long-curved handle, dip it in the large milk can and fill up the empty pail in readiness for the next customer.

Milk was one of the most sort after commodities in Australian towns. The money Rita collected was stuffed into a money bag she wore around her waist.

The boys began to shape up to each other and move in circles. Their father stood between them and gave the usual talk about clean fighting, no punches to the back or beneath the waist line.

Max knew that Keith never listened. What he did know was that Keith was a windmill fighter and had little skills and little finesse. What he did have was power and determination to always win. If that meant fighting dirty then he would.

Max recalled one fight that was behind a hotel in Port Douglas when the boys were only teenagers. The kid Keith had picked on was clever and it didn't take long for him to have the upper hand. Keith went down three times much to the delight of all the onlookers who were locals.

Max was in Keith's corner and tried to stop the fight. "Let me throw in the towel and then we can get to hell out of here. He's too big, too strong, too clever for you."

"Not on your bloody life," slurred Keith who was showing signs of concussion. There's more than one pig to skin a way."

"Now you're talking gibberish you idiot, I'm throwing in the towel. It will only cost us a tenner on the wager but at least you'll live to fight another day."

"You touch that towel kid and I'll pulverise you into little grains of sand. Watch this!"

Keith took off at full flight straight at his adversary who was still crouching on his haunches waiting for the third round to be called.

Keith slammed into him and they both sprawled across the grass. Keith grabbed the kid's head and pulled it towards himself. He opened his mouth wide and bit into the ear.

The kid was shocked by the illegal tactics that he had no time to retaliate or to defend himself. He squealed in pain as Keith's teeth sunk deep into the fleshy part of the ear. Keith then began to shake his head vigorously and finally pulled away with the bleeding ear still between his teeth.

The audience was aghast and revolted by the bloody mess and the squealing. Some ran away, others began to dry wrench a few stood in total shock.

Keith spat the ear out, grabbed Max by the arm, snatched up the £10 note that was sitting under a stone nearby and said, "Run like hell."

Max was too shocked to do any more than carry out the order. As he tore around the corner of the pub and out into the main street, he could hear police whistles being blown and two coppers ran past heading towards where the pandemonium appeared to be.

The boys reached the end of the street and ran on to the wharf where Keith carried Max clear into the water. They swam back under the jetty and hid there until night fall.

That was how Keith would operate if he felt he was losing. He was one mean bastard when he wanted to be.

"Okay, box," said Burton and his two boys began to shoot out short jabs at each other. Keith was a natural right hander holding his right against his body, cocked ready to explode into his opponent's face. The left hand he held out straight to protect himself and to shoot short jabs into the opponent's midriff.

Max was unusual as he was right-handed but displayed traits of being ambidextrous. Boxing was one of these. He was a south paw using his right hand to jab and protect and his left to inflict the stinging bunches to the head.

The boys kept circling and little was happening so Burton tried goading them. He loved nothing better than a good fight and he himself was handy with his fist.

Nowadays he was getting too long in the teeth and didn't have as many as he did when he was younger.

"Do you want me to put on some music? This is more like a waltz. Come on Maxy hold your dress out and swing around a few times."

Max didn't buy the goading but Keith did and he launched himself with his trade mark windmilling.

Max was ready and swayed out of the road of many of the punches. He was willing to take a few as long as it tired Keith and then he might get a hit or two into the right places.

One of the whirl wind blows had hit Max on the left cheek and split his lip so blood was pouring out. This gave Keith a renewed belief that he had his young brother on the ropes.

Max licked his lip and tasted the warm, salty liquid. He waited for the next onslaught with his head bowed as though he was spent. He noted Keith's heavy breathing and that both his arms had fallen to his side.

Keith didn't see the right jab that hit him squarely in the solar plexus. He felt the air explode from his lungs and felt himself double over.

Max then delivered the coup de grace. He swung his left hand down then up coming into Keith's jaw with a bone crunching uppercut.

Keith looked, glaze eyed and unbelieving and slowly toppled forward. Burton caught him and slowly lay him on the grass then turned him on his side.

"That's enough," said Marion and she stomped off towards the kitchen. She had to get prepared for the visitors that were on their way.

Within the hour of the fight ending the family heard engines roaring along the farm road and four cars and two motorcycles appeared. Dust was billowing behind the lead vehicle and all the others were blinded. The convoy came to a halt outside the home paddock and out jumped carload after car load of young soldiers all dressed in their khaki uniforms.

Marion hurried to meet them. "You must be Keith's mates come in, come in."

The first fellow forward was tall and rangy with an air of confidence. He slipped his arm through Marion's and called back to the others who were still tumbling out of cars or hopping off the motorcycles. "Come on lads this is the invite we were promised. By the way where's our host?"

"He's resting up on the sofa. Come along there's plenty to drink and eat. Start introducing yourselves to all of us. I'm Marion and this is my husband, Burton."

The introductions took some time but it was clear that the boys hungered for the alcohol and Keith's pretty sisters. There were lots of giggles and furtive kisses on cheeks as the morning wore on.

Marion was somewhat taken back by the number of men and the noise they created and when she finally aroused Keith from his concussion, she told him so. "I really only expected two or three mates not the 21 we have ended up with. They have taken over the house and are giving your sisters an embarrassing time. Will you kindly get them moving back to barracks?"

Keith staggered to his feet and set out to find the ringleader of the group. This was Glaston the very same man who had been the first to greet Marion. Keith took him aside and after a time there were nods of agreement.

Glaston yelled out over the top of the noise, "We need to be going boys so drink up the drink, kiss the girlies goodbye and collect the beer from the cooler."

There was a scramble to carry out the orders and it was not too long before the cars were loaded and the convoy sped and weaved its way out of the farm and over the mountains.

"Next time Keith can you please keep the number of your guests to less than four. A big group like that and any amount of trouble could break out," said Marion.

Max had strutted around the visitors feeling rather proud that he had finally not taken a beating from his older brother and to cap it off had actually beaten him. He didn't talk about it as that was not his way, preferring to internalize his victories and pat himself on the back. He was not one who needed the public accolades to grow and mature.

In his wanderings and drinking he came across the two bikers who had ridden up in the dust behind the cars.

"You know who owns the Triumph out the back, kid?" asked the larger of the two and the one with tattoos on every visible part of his skin.

"That's mine," said Max. "Got it for a song from a couple of blokes who live in Tully."

"You got done mate. Those two pinched the bike and find an unsuspecting soldier to flog it to?" said the thinner man as he took out a red and brown handkerchief and wiped his bald pate.

Max noticed he also had a tattoo and it was of an eagle in flight inked on the back across his shoulders. The head and beak stuck out from the collar of the man's shirt.

"Sorry to tell you mate but these two have been doing the rounds of the army camps and towns for months. They pinch bikes, change a few things and add a bit of paint then flog them off to unsuspecting blokes like you. What did you pay for it 90 bucks?"

"No cost 125 which I thought was pretty good. Goes like a charm, reaches 75mph and corners smoothly. Never had a worry since I paid for it."

"It's coming I can assure you," said the big guy who had been called King Tat by another soldier who had walked in and offered schooners to each of the three.

"You see most of the bikes they pinch they thrash to get away and to prove how good they are to prospective buyers. This then puts too much pressure on the chain and the back wheel sprocket and eventually throws them slightly out of alignment.

"You can be roaring along the road without a care and the chain will slip and grind into the sprocket. The back wheel seizes and the bike stops abruptly flinging you over the handlebars. If you live to walk again the bike will be a total write off."

"Shit," said Max, "You're not pissing me are you?"

"No mate on the straight and level. See this scar," and he lifted the front of his grey flannel singlet, "That's what happened to me when I fell for the buy me cheap trick. Had no idea it was coming. If I was you, I would get rid of the beast as soon as I could.

"In the meantime, get yourself all geared up for safety. I might add it's better to have one of those leather helmets, goggles, bandana around the mouth and a full suit of leather to take any spill you might have. Oh yes get a strong pair of leather boots with high zip up sides.

"Won't stop you from breaking your neck if you flip or run smack into a tree but it will lessen the lacerations and broken bones."

The party started to break up at this point so Max wandered down the back to check out the Triumph 100 Tiger. He didn't believe the two bruisers but he sure as hell wasn't going to suggest they were telling him lies.

He reckoned they were trying to get a bargain by bringing the bike into disrepute.

He sure thought they would be lying in wait for him in the next big town ready to take the dangerous machine off him for 50 bucks.

He approached the bike from the rear and got onto his haunches and lined up the huge sprocket. It was well over ten inches across. Further along under the seat he could see the gear sprockets. "Jesus," he said aloud, "They are all slightly out of alignment and some of the teeth are bent. This is a disaster."

He spent several days and hours working on getting the bike exactly right. His mechanic skills had gone up a peg or two.

Keith left the farm two days later. He was heading back to barracks and getting ready for his first trip overseas. There had been talk of setting up a forward Ambulance Corps on Bouganville Island.

Marion had wept her heart out even though Keith kept reassuring her he wouldn't be in the fighting. Marge clung to him and in the end, he practically dragged her on his foot to the car that he owned and drove. Eventually Burton had extricated Marge and carried the nine-year-old kicking and screaming back to her bedroom where he threw her through the door holus-bolus and key locked the door.

In the meantime Max continued to dream about joining the army and becoming a top soldier. He spent a lot of his waking hours counting the days he had to endure on the farm before he would be signing his Attestation Form.

As soon as he turned 18 Max intended to be at the door of the Kenmore Recruitment Centre to get an Attestation Form.

He had handed the form to his father one evening and after a simmering argument his father grudging approved. Burton had no option but to agree to anything that Max asked for. He had committed the worst crime possible on his son by calling him a liar and then thrashing him when he was nine year's old.

He could never forgive himself; he could never apologise to the boy so the next best thing was to give in to his demands and requests.

Max happily ran off to the Recruitment Centre and handed the form to a broad-shouldered soldier dressed in the khaki colours of the Australian Army.

On his shoulders he had the three chevrons of a sergeant.

"Well done son, all filled out and ready to help your fellow mates." It was a booming voice but one that made Max feel immensely proud of what he was about to embark upon. "You will be picked up here by bus tomorrow and be taken to the train station and from there to Puckapunyal for training. Go home, say your goodbyes and I'll see you in the morning."

With Max's mind made up he went home to break the news to the family.

All of the girls assembled in the lounge room that night for a special message from their father. They finished dinner before cleaning up and strolled into the lounge room.

Burton, their father came in last with Max slightly in front of him. Burton asked everyone to sit down. He then told them he was a very proud father because his youngest son had signed up with the army. Max added that he was doing this for the country and for the family.

Some of the audience began to weep and ask Max to reconsider. He was not going to budge as his mind was made up.

The next twenty-four hours flew past and Max found himself at Puckapunyal ready for his swift training and then a move into New Guinea to fight the Japanese.

∽∾

He soon discovered that army training was a lot of discipline like cleaning your uniform until all the brass ware shone. Making your bed without wrinkles and so that a 2/- florin would bounce off the sheets. Lots of marching and learning the drills. Understanding about rifles and submachine guns and keeping these clean and oiled. Hours and hours of being trained in hand-to-hand combat which included bayonet practice.

Max learnt to attach his double-edged bayonet to his rifle and charge a scarecrow stuffed with hay. The object was seen as the enemy so it was required that the soldiers had to stab the bayonet into the scarecrow, withdraw it and stab again.

The training also involved being de-humanised and Max soon learnt that he was there to kill or be killed.

In the meantime Max continued to dream about a top soldier. He spent a lot of his waking hours counting the days he had to endure the fierce training at Puckypunual.

Max found it hard to keep mates especially ones he called close. The thrashing he got from his father, when he was nine years old and the family lived in the Daintree, and all the lies that Keith told and got away with left him bereft of trust.

He and Keith had always been close with their older sibling, Burt. The other two kept an eye out for him and learnt so much of growing up and staying safe. Burt was a mentor and when he became the manager of his own trucking business the two youngsters were very proud of him.

The day the crocodile launch smashed Max's belief in closeness and he would rather run a thousand miles from someone rather than take up their offer of a schooner or a quiet chat in the beer garden. He knew it would take someone or something special to even get a tiny piece of that trust back. So, in the mean-time he avoided others unless it was work related.

He had shied away from everyone around the Daintree and the other towns the family was travelling through. His mind was totally filled with being a soldier and doing his bit for the country and the World.

Chapter 9

Bryan Bell came as a complete surprise into Max's life. To look at him you would dismiss him as an idiot and a baby-faced coward. He sauntered, head down, into Puckapunyal a few days after Max got there.

The guards had pointed out his barracks and the first person he tripped over on his way up the steps was Max. "Who the shit are you?" bellowed a furious Max who had cannoned into this skinny, freaky-looking kid. Both were sprawled on the steps looking at each other, one in sheer anger and the other pleadingly searching for directions.

"Private Bryan Bell, QX 41244," he stammered and adjusted the spectacles back onto the bridge of his nose. The lens glass was thick, really thick and it seemed to Max that the poor bugger would be stone blind without them. The kid bounded to his feet and saluted while calling his rank, name, and serial number.

Max slowly gained his feet and started to laugh. It was a deep, merry laugh one that he had hardly heard uttered from his mouth for over a decade. He looked again at the boy soldier and burst into another round of laughter.

"You don't have to be so rude I'm here as a new recruit. Can you kindly direct me to barrack C, bunk 47, please."

Max's instincts kicked in and he remembered his mother's constant motto, or was it a prayer, as she was always talking to her God. "I shall pass through this way but once. If I can do anything good for a fellow human I must do it now," or words to that effect.

"Sorry mate," he said and extended his hand. The grip from Bryan was surprisingly firm and as he pulled Max to his feet the upper arm strength was noticeable. He wasn't just a skinny little boy soldier he had an inner strength that belied his physical appearance.

Max showed the newbie his bunk and explained camp rules and then took Bryan on a tour. The boy was most grateful and said so a dozen times. By the time they got back to the barracks all the other members of the platoon were showering and getting dressed for dinner.

❦

Max introduced Bryan by yelling above the clatter and most nodded or said, "Hi ya."

From that day on Max felt he'd run into a trustworthy mate and one he could put his life in his hand. Sometimes you get things right other times you miss by the proverbial mile. This was going to be one of the former.

The barracks was full to overflowing with 32 men bunked down in a Nissan Hut built for 25 so tempers at times were short and the constant arguing over space was annoying to Max. He had bunk 26 which he thought was rather lucky as he had been born in Rockhampton on June 4th, 1926. He kept his area spotless as his mother had taught him and was always complimented and used as an example by the staff sergeant when it was inspection time.

They managed to get three proper bastards amongst their platoon. At that moment Bullfrog or Lance Corporal Smythe was laying on his bunk with a white towel wrapped around his waist. He had flicked the join into a position so that his dick was showing to all and sundry.

Spider Wilson, a skinny little bloke who loved to smoke cigarettes sat on the bed and was rubbing the penis up and down. Standing above the two was Horse or Private Clyde S Dale. He was waiting expectantly for his turn at manipulating the distended penis.

"Gently, gently we don't want the snake to hiss too soon. That is just right. Here, give Horse a turn. Brylcream yourself first then finish me off."

Everyone in the barracks ignored the carry-on that went on every night with one or the other being ejaculated by the others. Sometimes they managed to get two going at one time.

As soon as they had finished all three would bound for the loo, order everyone out and slam the door. Odd sounds would continue for a few minutes and then the showers got turned on full bore.

Bryan had been warned by Max about these shenanigans and told to ignore anything he thought weird or odd in the barracks. "Remember old son these blokes are living on borrowed time and could be dead by morning so they are going to do anything or take ridiculous risks that they might not take in peace time."

Max had taken Bryan for a stroll one evening and gave him some vital advice. "Keep your eyes averted and your ears gummed up and most of all keep your mouth shut tight. You need to be a wise monkey, see no evil, hear no evil and speak no evil."

Luckily for Bryan his bunk was up the other end from the three bully boys so he was well into bed before they started their weird acts.

The next afternoon the platoon was sent to the Rifle Range for target practice. There was no need for this as they had all been shooting targets twice a day for weeks. Added to that all of them had passed with flying colours and could hit a florin at 200 yards.

Everything in the army was regimented. You were given an order you carried it out, no questions, no arguments. Sometimes Max would stand in sheer frustration listening to an officer of rank give an order that was pure bullshit and lacked any practicality or common sense.

Into the breach would march the platoon or sometimes it was the whole battalion. Then after being massacred by the 'pretend' Japanese Army the referees would call the war games to a halt and point out everyone was dead at least three times over and that they were a mob of sitting, fucking ducks.

In the end, Max just did as he was told and waited for the inevitable. No wonder the poor bastards at Gallipoli were mown down like sheaves of wheat. "Over the top go, go on the whistle." And the Turks would open up with machine guns. Didn't anyone have the good sense to try and sneak around behind or to one side or whatever?

"Just carry out your commands Johnson that's what you're here for. No heroes wanted and none expected."

The usual betting and tomfoolery went on across the hour as man after man stepped up to fire his obligatory five rounds. After each had shot the call would come down, "Five bulls."

After all the soldiers had wasted 40 rounds having been up to the plate eight times the platoon was dismissed back to barracks.

Max was glad that the shooting was over as the recoil of the old 303 was nasty and left ugly purple bruises on his shoulder. He sidled up to Bryan and thumped him on his right shoulder. There was a sharp cry of pain and Max knew that Bryan was also suffering from the recoil.

Max was content telling Bryan about the other training he would be undertaking. He got carried away explaining the best parts of his training was twofold.

First was going on bivouacs where you walk for miles, set up camp and stay overnight.

In the morning you packed up and walk back to barracks. To make things more war like there were booby traps set along the way and ambushes at every corner.

Second, being a forward scout. In Max's experiences he had on numerous times saved his platoon which was out gunned from ambushes. Due to Max's diligence and sharp decision making he had saved his platoon.

Durng the telling of his experiences so far Max noticed Bryan rubbing his right shoulder. He said to the kid, "Let's take a look." Bryan obliged and as his sleeve was lifted Max could see the tell-tale blueness of the bruising. "Get some cold water onto that it will stop the internal bleeding."

Bryan pulled the sleeve back down and the two mates high tailed it to the barracks.

Three weeks of rifle range practice was enough to start complaining. Max was a top scoring shooter so found the exercise stimulating but boring all together. He was of the opinion that the men should have been involved in other real life target shooting. To him it was not likely that a soldier creeping through the jungles of New Guinea would be shooting at a target 500 yards away while laying on the ground.

Max tried to argue this point with the Range Sergeant but was told that he was required to obey his commander at every command. "But sir you can't see more than five yards in the rainforest and secondly you would need to be firing bullets from the hip as you fling yourself onto the ground. The outburst of fire gives your position away instantly so you need to be able to spin and roll while firing."

The answer he received was full pack and twenty laps of the parade ground.

∽o∽

One evening after being dismissed from target shooting Max heard his name called by the Sergeant. He looked at Bryan and said, "Here I go again. You go back to the barracks and settle in and I'll be along after my laps."

Max turned and marched double pace to the Sergeant. "What's the go sarge wasn't my 40 out of 40 good enough?"

"Too good and that's where you get a new assignment. The jungles of the Pacific are a different theatre of war than anything we have ever fought in.

"Your experience in the Daintree rainforest makes you the ideal fighting man in the jungle environs. Not only are you astute as a forward scout but you pick up sights and sounds the rest of us know nothing about.

"Now here is the order from Colonel Bright and it is directed specifically to you. He will be on site tomorrow to watch you carry out what he hopes will be a method to put the Japs on the back foot during ambushes. Are you up to it or do I need to find another man?"

"I am your man sir just outline the plan and I'll give it my best shot."

∞

Max was first off the truck at Barron Falls and marched over to Colonel Bright. He saluted and said, "You wanted to see me sir."

Colonel Bright replied, "Yes Johnson I have a plan for you that I believe will give our fighting men a chance to out fox the Jap snipers and their ambushes.

"What we need is a flanker with each platoon who can ride the high side and bring to bear accurate shots to 1000 yards. That will take the heat off any platoon caught out and give them time to withdraw or plan an assault.

"The Jap machine gun emplacements and their snipers are cutting our boys to ribbons. The range sergeant guarantees that you can hit a target 40 out of 40 at 1000 yards. You show me you can do that shooting with accuracy you get the job.

"It's not a matter of laying on a blanket and shoot. This test will be right here in the jungle area near Barron Falls and will start in the next 15 minutes. You got his soldier or not?"

"I've got it sir," replied Max and saluted.

∞

The Lieutenant took an eight-man squad up to the Barron Falls and set out simulating a Jap ambush with 3 machinegun emplacements and two snipers in trees.

He took the rest of the men, including Max, some half a mile away from the falls and set out the plan. Max was to be the left point, up the slope and moving at 1000 yards from the main group.

He switched off soon after hearing his role as he knew all too well that the plan was ridiculous. He lived in the Daintree for ten years and was aware of the terrain and environment from aged 0 to 10.

Anyone who had set foot off the clearing or track into the rainforest environment wouldn't be able to see squat within two yards of their position. He wanted to argue the point but the officers knew what they were doing and the privates were only required to carry out the commands.

He allowed his mind to wander and he began to pick up the sounds and smells around him. "What a perfect place for an ambush," he thought. "Bet these officers haven't got a clue as to why they have found such an ideal place to take out an enemy's whole platoon."

Chapter 10

Max begun to count off the clues as to why this was a perfect place to set an ambush "The waterfall was a few hundred yards further up the river and the sound it made as the massive amounts of water tumbled 60 yards shut out all other noises.

As a scout you would have no warning signs that you were walking into a trap. The denseness of the jungle made it impossible to see more than a few yards ahead or to the left or right. Funny how scouts go through the checks before moving their platoons forward when one of the most important places to check is behind. Many an enemy would wait for a scout to pass by before sneaking forward and slitting their throats."

As he waited patiently for all the others to be briefed his eyes wandered to the magnificent falls that cascaded over 60 yards from the rocky outcrops and crashed onto the valley floor below. The noise was thunderous and the spray was caught in the sunlight creating beautiful rainbows.

All about, trying to catch the tiny sprays of water were huge, dark blue, Ulysses butterflies. The Ulysses butterfly (*Papilio ulysses*) is a large swallow tail butterfly of Australia with a wingspan of up to four inches.

"Johnson, let's get the show on the road. They reckon you're quick so let's give you five minutes to be in place. Go!" bawled the Lieutenant.

Max swung his 303 rifle onto one shoulder and set off at a cracking pace. He didn't run straight up but rather began to seek out the natural contours, twisting this way and that, all the time climbing in an upward movement.

He counted as he climbed and gulped in the cool fresh air. He had learnt as a kid to count by seconds to know how long he had been under the water when he and his brothers and Andy were duck diving in the Daintree River.

It had been fun as well as a fierce competition to see who could stay under the longest. Andy, being the eldest and the more experienced always won hands down. He held the record of 3 minutes 47 seconds whereas Max had to surface, gasping at 2 minutes 22 seconds. Nevertheless, it had taught Max how to keep regular time and to get to 300 he knew he was right on the 5 minute allowance.

He was by now high up on the ridge and looking down to where the brigade would be waiting. As he guessed he couldn't see anyone or anything except for the trees and undergrowth of the forest.

This was going to be a pointless exercise. He had no option but to carry out his part as set out by the Lieutenant.

∞o∞

Fifteen minutes later Max heard the first of the machine guns chattering and spitting their deadly lead at his unsuspecting mates. He cut back down the hill, running fast and in a direct line to the sound. He ducked and weaved, taking small, rapid steps to keep his balance and avoid the tree trunks. Anyone of the objects in his path could have brought him undone or even knocked him unconscious.

∞o∞

The stinging nettle was his worst enemy and his vigilance for this curse was at its height. Next came Wait-a-while another damn painful creeper that could stop you in your tracks, clinging to every part of your uniform and bringing you to a halt.

∞o∞

The machine guns were still firing rapidly as Max neared the path that ran through this part of the forest. He knew the nests were about 30 yards ahead and he caught glimpses of his comrades pinned down among the vegetation of the forest floor.

He stayed off the track and advanced quickly and stealthily past the machine gunners. He turned behind them and came in quickly towards the first gun.

He heard the tell-tale clicking of a jammed gun so he leapt over the gunners and fired into the second nest which was still slamming rounds into the platoon that was pinned down.

Max swivelled around and rushed the first machinegun nest and took out the two gunners just before they got the gun unjammed and firing again. He picked up the heavy machine gun from foxhole two and turned it at the third machine gun.

They could only fire forward and that gave Max time to cut them to ribbons with the machine gun he had hefted to his hip and pulled the trigger. He continued to fire and move the gun in an arc to cut down the two snipers. They were also facing forward and didn't have time to swivel their weapons towards Max.

"Well done Private Johnson," came a shout back through the forest. "That worked a treat." It was the Lieutenant rushing forward to take the accolades for his well-prepared plan.

"Total fuck up and the worst plan ever devised," yelled Max who completely lost it. "I was so far in the jungle I couldn't see anything, couldn't offer any guidance or protection to my mates. Don't start big mouthing your stupid bloody plan. If I hadn't run like a maniac, following the machine gun sounds and then had the good sense to get in behind then you would all be chewed to bits by now."

"Ah but as the flanker you saved the day so the plan has merit. A little tweak here and there and we'll surprise the shit out of those Japs," retorted the Lieutenant.

'Oh, for Chrissake let's go home," said an exasperated Max. He picked up his rifle and trudged passed his comrades. Each patted him on the back and offered to buy him a beer or two back at camp.

The revised plan had to wait for two days as there was an urgent call to the parade ground when the squad got back to the Tully Barracks.

In fact, the security sergeant on the gate ordered the truck driver to go straight to the parade ground. The message was delivered loud and clear. The Battalion would be moving to Lae within the week so get prepared.

Max was still seething about the new plan and wanted desperately to tell the Lieutenant what he believed would be a better way to look after the men in a jungle environment.

Max and Bryan were always in each other's company. When they heard the news, they were being shipped to Lae they agreed to look after each other.

Max was concerned that his mate's conscience would get him into more trouble than it was worth. He sat Bryan down to him talk to him. He turned to Bryan gave him a push and offered some astute advice, "Head down old son, be all wise like the monkey and keep your thoughts to yourself. That especially goes for when those three galoots we have in the hut. They are bad news at the best of times and evil when provoked."

Max sent Bryan back to the hut one evening as he had been called to headquarters. Bryan had made it safely back but was one of the stragglers.

As he came through the door, he saw Spider was stark naked and lying on his belly. Bullfrog was easing the cheeks of his backside out and running a finger smeared with Brylcreem into his anus. He began to increase the movement as Bryan drew near.

Bryan forgot all he had been told and stopped. He glared and blurted out loudly, "You filthy pair of bastards."

Bullfrog sprang from the kneeling position on the bed and grabbed Bryan by the throat. He was remarkably quick for such a big man with a beer gut that hung well over his belt.

"What did you call me little man?" he spat the words into Bryan's face and squeezed the throat tighter. Bryan couldn't reply and he knew that he was about to breathe his last on earth.

Bullfrog was furious and his face was bright red and the bald patch on his head dripping with sweat.

"Horse, bring the rifle and the Vaseline and follow me. Now." He emphasised 'now' and the whole hut shuddered.

Every pair of eyes were looking into a pillow or hands were sweeping at nothing under a bed. Bullfrog lifted the limp body of Bryan by the grip on his throat and carried him bodily into the showers.

Spider grabbed his towel, wrapped it around himself and like an expectant little boy at Christmas rushed off to follow.

The door was slammed after the last of those who had been showering were expelled. There was one muffled scream. Cut short and nothing more except the full blast of the showers and the basin taps.

Nearly half an hour past before Bullfrog, Spider and Horse emerged with towels wrapped around their waist, singing and giggling as though nothing had happened. Everyone in the hut pretended to be asleep.

An hour later Max wandered in and began to get ready for a quick shower. He tried to be very quiet as it was well after lights out. He reached the shower and was surprised to see blood dribbling from the urinal area. This was hidden further away from the open showers.

Chapter 11

He ventured along and was shocked to find Bryan lying in the pool of urine, stark naked and bleeding from his backside. Max felt his heart melting and he whispered, "What have they done to you, my little man?"

He helped Bryan into a sitting position and then lifted him up. He used the fireman's lift to get the lad over his shoulder and he quietly carried him to his bunk. He laid him on his back then rolled him onto his side.

Max was concerned at the amount of blood leaking from Bryan's rear. He went across to his own bed and found three handkerchiefs ironed into squares. He went back to Bryan and eased the bottom of his cheeks open and pushed the handkerchiefs into the space. These would stem the flow of blood for a while and hopefully help the congealing to begin.

He covered the naked body with the sheet and blankets and said a silent prayer. "God if you are real help Bryan and get the bastards who did this." He didn't have any belief in this God bloke but he would change his mind in a few days.

The next morning everything in the barracks seemed to be normal. Soldiers were up and polishing brass, blackening boots and belts, scrubbing teeth, and talking quietly to each other. Bryan was awake and dressed and cleaning his rifle. Inspection was seconds away when Max finally finished making his bed. He stood to attention at the foot of the stretcher and glimpsed over to Bryan. The lad was standing to attention and the only thing that looked a little odd was his right trouser pocket bulged as though he had three or or more handkerchiefs stuffed in it.

After inspection the platoon was dismissed to have a quiet morning. Lunch was to be at 1200 hours and then they would be addressed on the parade ground at 1300 hours.

Max grabbed a bottle of beer and half a packet of milk arrowroot biscuits and ran after Bryan who had left the hut alone. As he approached from behind it was obvious that the lad was limping badly although back at the hut he seemed to be alright.

"What the hell happened to you? I turn my back for five minutes and you fall over in the shower?" said Max.

"If that's all it was, I'd be a happy boy but it was more than that. I should have remembered your words about keeping my mouth shut, eyes averted and ears plugged. But I couldn't."

"Come on buddy," said Max. "Let's escape to the other side of the parade ground and we'll have a little morning tea and you can fill me in."

"I think a 303 barrel was enough to fill me in for life thanks very much," said Bryan.

"What are you talking about? Come on over to that big tree and you can tell me what happened."

Bryan kept talking about his ordeal as they wandered across the barren, sandy parade ground. By the time they reached the cedar that grew luxuriously Max was seething. "They raped you with the rifle barrel?"

"Yes, because I wouldn't comply with their demands to lay still and open my buttocks. Horse was on top of my head belting it every time I refused. Spider had one leg and that stinking Bullfrog had the other. Bullfrog was trying to keep my legs apart and enter at the same time but there was no way I was going to let him. Finally, they gave up, picked up the rifle, put a clip in, slid a bullet into the breech and said, "Either the barrel goes in or the bullet take your pick."

"I took the barrel and it hurt like hell. Those bastards have fooled with the very last person they will ever fool with on this earth. They are dead," said Bryan vehemently.

Max had never heard anyone speak with such hatred and feared for his mate and the three targets.

∾o∾

After lunch, Max took Bryan back to the hut as his wounds were bleeding. He got some more of his handkerchiefs and took Bryan into one of the toilet cubicles. He was aghast at the bruising around the anus and the bleeding that was coming from deeper inside.

He said, "We need to get you to the doctor as this is not stopping. You don't know how much internal damage has been done. We'll make up a story and get you seen to."

Bryan was getting weaker and the pain was almost unbearable, so he agreed.

∽o∽

Max was busy filling in the nurse as to how Bryan came to have a badly bruised and bleeding anus while the doctor examined the area and kept shaking his head. "Yes falling onto a wooden stake bum first would cause a laceration and bruising. It must have been rather sharp and penetrated nearly a foot inside. I assume he has had a new pair of trousers issued."

"Yes sir," assured Max.

"He will need to stay here a while until I can get the bleeding to stop. My biggest concern is the colon appears to be perforated and this will mean leakage of the intestines into the body causing septicaemia. When this happens, he will only have days to live."

Max was shocked to hear the prognosis but Bryan became all business like. "I need to get moving."

∽o∽

The Colonel stood at attention on the dais awaiting the final group to take up their positions. He stepped forward and announced in a loud, clear voice, "You will embark on the Gardinia at 0430 hours at the Brisbane dock tomorrow morning and from there be disembarked in Lae, New Guinea. The Japs are on a full-scale push down the east coast of New Guinea and through the centre along the Kokoda trail. You will stop them and send them packing. That is your mission; do not fail your country and your families."

Everyone made haste back to their barracks where they had to pack lightly, catch forty winks and be ready to climb aboard a truck at 2200 hours next morning. There was the constant clicking and clinking of metal as 303s were dismantled, cleaned, oiled and re-assembled.

Bryan was in agony with his anus but was pretending to be strong. Max wandered over to offer sympathy and help. "How's it going my little mate?" he asked.

"So, so but bloody agonizing," said Bryan as he stuffed a pair of khaki trousers into his duffel bag. He pulled on the cord to do it up and tied a knot to stop anything falling out.

"You been back to the doctor this afternoon?" asked Max.

"Nah, he told me yesterday it was a waste of time. My only chance is to have a full scale operation and even that might be too late. Anyway, I have a far more important mission to see carried out."

"You are a bloody fool but I love you," said Max as his eyes welled with tears. "Just remember I've got your back so anything you need let me know."

"All's good just keep a watch on my back like you offered and I'll be fine." There was something strange in the way Bryan said that final sentence but Max couldn't quite put his finger on it. Come what may he would stay right behind Bryan and keep him alive for as long as possible. Maybe, just maybe, he could find a good surgeon at the Lae Field Ambulance and persuade Bryan to have the operation he desperately needed.

∽o∽

The night was short and the sleep was restless for all the men in the Nissan hut. Four thirty came all too soon and then all hell seemed to break loose as men dressed, packed, showered, farted and ran. Eventually all soldiers were lined up in full kit behind their allotted trucks.

Fortune smiled as someone had insisted the canvas covers be placed over the steel structures thus making a waterproof canopy. The scudding clouds across the moon presaged a torrential downpour at any second. Tully was a wet place in winter so when it rained it poured for hours.

Bryan sat next to Max holding his rifle between his legs and his duffel bag at his feet. There were a good 50 men packed like sardines inside the canopy and this was one of thirty trucks so it was a huge move of over 1500 soldiers.

Just as the engines began to fire the canvas near Max's left ear was yanked up and the camp doctor stood close by. "Is Bryan with you? Good. Here's some antiseptic ointment and a tin of antibiotic powder. Help him put it on the wound and get him to push it in as far as his finger can reach. It won't cure him but will give a little relief and a few extra days. I really would have preferred him to remain in camp. Best of luck you plucky little bugger."

The canvas was pulled shut and the truck lurched forward and stopped. The driver had stalled the truck in the cold morning. Max smiled as he recalled his first truck driving lesson all those years ago. Big brother Burt had put him behind the wheel, turned on the motor, explained how the gears and clutch worked and set him ready. Max had yanked his foot off the clutch, slammed the accelerator down and the truck launched forward and then abruptly stopped. Max was thrown violently forward and flung backwards causing a whiplash of his neck. "Stalled the bugger," was all Burt said before he burst out laughing.

At the back of the truck the flap was opened slightly and a hand with no body launched a pill bottle into the crowd. Some smart lackey called, "Grenade," and everyone laughed.

From outside Max heard the doctor call out, "That's for Private Bryan Bell. They're pain killers, he'll need them."

The truck moved away, took its place in the mile long convoy and began to pick up pace.

"Next stop Brisbane then somewhere in New Guinea," thought Max. "How many of us will return alive," he wondered.

∞o∞

The trip into Brisbane and onto the Gardinia went smoothly although it was a miracle how they got all 1500 men onto the ship as quickly as they did. Breakfast of bacon, eggs and baked beans was served in relays by a huge crew of chefs and then everyone was told to settle down wherever they could. There were a few squabbles over best places to bunk down but as the trip was less than two days it seemed pointless to use energy up on pettiness rather than keep it for the real enemy.

∞o∞

Lae was a coastal town on the east side of New Guinea and had been overrun several times by the Japs before the Americans and then the Aussies had wrestled it back. It was now a thriving settlement armed to the teeth and ready to resist the expected advancing Jap army.

The Gardinia swept passed the town and its bustling harbour and continued along the coast. Bryan looked at Max and said, "Where the hell are we off to. I thought it was Lae."

"All that jungle training we did puts us further north where the main Jap Imperial Army has supposed to set up a secret staging post. They've hidden it in the jungle and it includes an aerodrome as well. We are going to disrupt the push and set the little bastards packing back home."

"Just hope I can last that long," said Bryan as he moved his weight from the left buttock to the right.

"You're holding up remarkably well old son. I'm real proud of you."

The platoon sergeant Butcher sidled up to Max and said, "We are going in by landing craft north of where the others are to decamp. We draw the short straw to do reconnaissance of this phantom Jap base everyone keeps talking about. No noise, no shooting, just in and then out.

"We make our way the 20 miles south to the staging area. Top secret so no uniforms, no insignia and all dog tags to be given to the ship's purser before leaving. Be ready in ten."

"Right sergeant I'll help gather up the platoon," said Max. "Shit," he thought, "If we get caught they'll shoot us as spies and we'll disappear into the unknown. What the hell is this all about?"

Bryan picked up his rifle and duffel bag and began to follow. "Not you man, you won't make it half way with that bum of yours."

"I'm not missing this for all the tea in China," and he pushed past Max and made for the landing craft that was being lowered by the forward derrick. A rope ladder was flung over the side and secured to the hand rails. Men began clambering over the edge.

Bryan smiled a cruel smile as he noted with satisfaction that Bullfrog and Horse were clambering into the boat. He swung a leg over the railing and worked his way down the rope ladder.

As he settled in a seat at the back, he nodded happily to himself as Snake came with a rush into the bottom of the boat. "All three how much better could this get!"

They landed on a remote beach full of pebbles and Max made the observation that it couldn't have been a Queensland one as that would have been full of golden sand. The landing craft pulled away and was soon lost in the darkness. They were alone and had no back-up so they needed to search fast and quiet and get to hell out of there before they stirred a hornets' nest.

Instructions had already been issued and everyone set off in twos and threes to reconnoitre their allotted areas. Once completed the whole group was to make for a tall Cocos palm on the southern extremity of the beach. They had no more than 75 minutes to complete their tasks and get to hell out of the area.

The darkness played tricks with everyone's vision but it soon became obvious that the Japs were in the area in numbers. There were wheel tracks and fallen trees as proof. Fox holes and trenches formed mazes in all directions but they were covered and deserted. It seemed that even if someone found the set up they would mistake it as abandoned.

The platoon didn't have time to push inland for four miles because if they did they would have found the small city of a battalion of Japanese soldiers.

Max took his contingent to sweep the northern area and found evidence that the Japs had been active from the beach to over a mile inland. The footprints and tracks of vehicles were less than a day old. He pushed his team to do the scouting and then moved them south to reconnoitre with the main group. As they approached the tall cocos tree an MLC came speeding into the beach and twenty or so soldiers piled out. The officer in charged called to Max, "Where's Butcher. There's a change of plan."

Max led the soldier to where he could just make out the figure of the tall sergeant. There was an exchange between the two men and then Sergeant Butcher approached Max to tell him he was to take the new group inland and work in an arc as the latest message placed the Japs in numbers somewhere in the jungle. The Navy had to have an accurate location to hit them hard with their guns. Max was to go with the officer who had just arrived to scout for him.

Max introduced himself and in turn the officer said, "Colonel Barry Devon with twenty men."

After consulting the map with Sergeant Butcher the three men worked out a path to move through and a place some twenty miles further south where they could meet up by 0600 hours. That would give Max six hours to cover the distance. There was to be no contact with the enemy as their strength was unknown.

Max set off at double time followed by the marines in the party.

Chapter 12

He moved well into the jungle and kept every-
one bunched up with two outriders and a tail-end
Charlie. He worked as forward scout with Colonel
Devon alongside.

The men had travelled quickly and quietly for an
estimated sixteen miles when Max called a halt and
indicated for the team to crouch, guns at the ready.
Ahead were several tall fig trees with spreading,
thick branches.

Several hours before a small patrol of Japanese had
rested under these same trees. The officer in charge
had decided to set a trap by placing two of his men
as snipers in the trees. The two nominees climbed a
tree each and found a sturdy limb to rest upon and to
settle their rifle on. They strapped themselves in so
that they made no noise even when their bodies came
under stress. The snipers would be picked up in the
morning and returned to base.

Colonel Devon waited patiently for the move on direction but it was a long time coming. Max had stayed stock still and every now and again he sniffed.

The Japanese snipers had been in the trees for over five hours when the first had the urge to urinate. He had opened his fly and tied a piece of creeper to his penis. The creeper was tied to another branch a yard to his right and two yards lower than where he was laying. In the course of having to pee he was trained to dribble the urine slowly out so it travelled along the creeper onto the branch below and drip to the ground.

The dripping sound was almost inconsequential but anyone who could hear the sound they would pinpoint a position that was of a phantom origin. The real maker of the sound was located two yards higher and to the left. The other sniper had a similar set up in another tree some 20 yards towards the beach.

Colonel Devon became agitated and said, "We must move on Private. I can't hear anything or see anything.

Max smiled and recalled his adventure into the Daintree to watch his big brother cavorting with girls. One came close to his hiding place and had to relieve herself. The smell was distinctive and it was the same smell he could smell now and directly ahead of the team, ammonium.

He whispered to Devon, "Someone has had a pee up that nearest fig tree and he's still there. I'm trying to pinpoint the position. I've also got another sniper to our right but need to get closer. Find me your two best shooters and bring them in quietly.

Max set up the first shooter and pointed to where he believed the Jap sniper was waiting. "Do you know the call of a Whipbird?"

Both men shook their heads and waited for a demonstration. Max wet his lips and whistled the double take of a whip bird's song. It sounded like a whip being cracked.

"That's the signal, so when you hear it open fire. Place at least five shots into the position I will give you." With that he pointed at the fig tree and whispered the location. He tapped the other shooter and began sneaking over towards the other tree.

He settled the soldier and then began to smell out the urine of the sniper. This one was easier because his relief was only recent and he had been somewhat lazy in not tying the creeper to the branch lower down. It swung a mere six inches in the breeze and was still dripping from his last pee. Max showed the shooter where he wanted the five bullets planted. He carefully pushed a magazine onto his own gun and sighted the location.

☙❧

It was nearly 0500 hours and the twilight was slowly illuminating parts of the forest. He wet his lips again and whistled the Whipbird's song. Simultaneously the rifles exploded and the rat-a-tat of the fifteen bullets followed.

Max waited for several minutes. He was sure he heard a grunt from his target but not the other. He wasn't doubting his ability but he didn't want any of the men hurt. He had to be sure that the snipers had been taken out. He called out in Japanese, "Guddoshotto Kenji", which translates to Good shot Kenji and waited. He repeated the call again before walking to the fig tree Thirty yards up the tree he could make out a large swelling on the limb, a sure sign that a foreign body was attached. He called to the Colonel who confirmed the other sniper was deceased.

The Colonel came rushing up and slapped Max on the back. "Private Johnson you just save my men's lives. Such clever skills."

The platoon arrived at the rendezvous point in time. The colonel couldn't help telling everyone how clever Max had proven to be and how he saved the twenty soldiers. He added that his group was under instruction to remain at the rendezvous position for the next week and watch for Japanese movements. They were not to engage the enemy and would be picked up by a passing naval vessel.

The colonel and sergeant separated the two groups. The sergeant set his full complement off at double pace to the south. They stopped for a rest just before dawn and tucked into bully beef and a crusty bun all supplied by the chefs on the ship before they disembarked. For a drink they had to suffice with the crystal-clear water of a creek which turned out to be surprisingly refreshing.

After an hour's rest and the sun lifting above the vast ocean to the east the soldiers under the command of Sergeant Butcher shouldered arms and set out for the staging camp. The sergeant wasn't expecting to have any problems ahead and had been lax in not setting a forward scout, flankers nor a tail end Charlie.

Max was not impressed but rather than pick an argument quietly went about setting up a classical platoon. Each of the men he chose nodded in acquiescence and moved to their allotted position. Bryan was walking a little ahead of Max who had placed himself in the centre of the group. This was where the sergeant should have been so as to direct commands should an attack occur. The sergeant was too busy, sharing a bottle of vodka that he had squirrelled from the larder in the ship, with Bullfrog, Spider and Horse.

Bryan was carrying a Tommy gun and had angled across so that he was several yards behind the foursome. He was carrying the gun at his hip but with the safety catch on.

Max kept pace with Bryan and was a little annoyed with the way he kept angling away from the path but put it down to his aching buttocks. He hoped he'd had time somewhere in the last few hours to sprinkle the powder on the anus and to take a painkiller or two.

Max noticed that the sergeant, and his entourage that he was entertaining, were approaching a fallen log that crossed the path and lay 60 yards into the forest. It wasn't the log that had caught his eyes but the bamboo shoots that were stuck at 5-yard intervals into the log. They stuck up about a foot and had green shoots on then. These raised an alarm with Max as bamboo shoots do not grow on tree trunks in this manner.

Max flashed his eyes forward and across searching for the tell-tale signs of either a sniper or a machinegun nest as it was just the thing either would set up as a sighter. As he looked he noticed the forward scout raise a fist and then fling himself onto the ground. Max screamed, "Hit the deck" and in the same instance lunged at Bryan. Just as he glanced off his mate's hip he heard the safety catch of the Tommy Gun flick off, the Jap machine gun started chattering and Bryan's Tommy Gun blasted away. On his way down Max saw to his horror that the Tommy gun was cutting through the Sergeant and his three companions from behind while the enemy machine gunner was spraying the platoon with bullets from the front.

Max hit the muddy ground hard and then Bryan landed on top of him. They were neck on neck with Bryan on top. Max could feel Bryan's pulse beating a rapid staccato and felt hot, sticky liquid flowing over his face and through his hair. It was his own blood, or that of Bryan, either way one or both were mortally wounded.

He didn't dare move.

The guns all seemed to stop at once and the sound of men speaking Japanese came from several directions. Max froze and waited for the inevitable. The throbbing of Bryan's pulse suddenly ceased and Max knew he'd lost his best friend. He held back the tears and kept his breathing as shallow as he could.

The first pistol shot rang out and the kicking of a body by heavy boots was heard not far away. Another shot echoed across the clearing. They were shooting the wounded and making sure no one was left alive. Max could play dead and hope or jump up and try to take a few out. He opted for the possum trick as Bryan's weight was too much to move in one bound. He had to hope they would see all the blood and believe he had copped a bullet or two across the skull, splitting it open.

Another shot rang out and then excited chattering and an Australian voice pleading, "I want to live please. I have two young kids at home."

It was one of the soldiers that Max was not readily acquainted with. He knew of him to say hi but didn't know his name. "Really weird that you can be so close to people but not know anything about them."

The pleading and crying continued.

Max couldn't see past the fallen log and was desperately trying to keep his pupils from moving so he could only guess what was happening. He heard broken English being spoken harshly and realised that a Jap officer had arrived. Officers had the reputation of being sadistic and cruel beyond imagination.

"Tie em up and I send em to Empra as gif."

"Oh my God no," thought Max, "They are going to behead the poor bastard." He felt his finger tighten slightly around the trigger of his 303 but stopped himself.

Then he heard the swish of a sword and the sickening clunk. It reminded Max of the wild pig hunts on the Daintree where someone was nominated to behead the pig with an axe. This sounded so brutal and revolting.

It took all Max's internal fortitude to hold back from dry wrenching and thus giving himself away.

He was virtually one stroke away from following his ill-fated comrade.

He could hear footsteps nearby and the thunk, thunk as the Japs kicked the corpses to see if any still lived. Any doubt was followed by a volley from a pistol. He felt Bryan's body gentling swaying and for a moment thought the lad still lived.

Chapter 13

It was a Jap soldier rocking the body with this boot. He felt a violent, stinging boot to his own right side ribs and felt one crack. The pain was unbearable and he felt he couldn't breathe.

He held his composure like his life depended on it and then heard the unmistakable click of a pistol. "Shit it must have misfired and I'm still alive," thought Max, He waited with his breath held for what seemed like an eternity.

He was sure he had beaten Andy's record for holding one's breath by double.

Slowly the voices and footfalls receded and the eerie silence of the wilderness took over. Even the usual chirrup of birds was missing and there was no breeze to stir the leaves. Max slowly let his breath out, staying as still as possible and waited.

⌘

He lay still, not moving all day. Darkness would be the only friend he could now rely on. The shooting and movement among the dead had ceased but Max knew better than to even twitch.

Max finally thought it was dark enough for him to wriggle out from under the dead weight of his friend. He raised his head ever so slightly and peered around. His night sight had clicked in so he could see quite well by the moonlight over about ten yards.

He crawled and dragged himself over body after body deeper into the jungle. Once he was surrounded by the thickness of the rainforest he knew he could outsmart and out manoeuvre any man so that's where he had to be.

How long it took to feel it was safe to stand and run he couldn't tell but once he made-up his mind he set off at a cracking pace.

A sentry challenged Max as he broke clear of the jungle and rushed towards the encampment, he could see in the dawn light. "Who goes there? Identify yourself or I'll shoot."

Max was taken through to the main tent where a temporary command post had been established and was surprised to find Brigadier Potts sitting at the table.

"Johnson isn't it? Heard a lot about you especially those years you spent in the Daintree. Must have been good training for you. Where the hell have you come from looking like death warmed up?"

Max spent an hour explaining all he remembered and cleverly left out those things that the brass didn't need to know. If there was one thing he learned after his thrashing in the Daintree by his father was, 'Once thrashed then forever lie', because people only believe what they want to believe anyway.

The one major mystery was how the Japs knew the platoon was on the track as they had positioned their machine gun nests facing away from where an expected attack should have come from. Was it pure luck, a mole on the ship, or had they simply become disoriented in the jungle? Unfortunately, these questions were never answered.

He left the meeting pleased with his report but saddened by the loss of his entire platoon. If only the sergeant had been more vigilant maybe they would have been alerted earlier.

He was pleased for Bryan as the cunning little bugger had got his revenge and the pain he was suffering was now gone forever.

He was devastated by what the Japs did to his wounded mates and now knew that this was a tough, uncompromising, and brutal enemy, one that had to be stopped at all costs.

∽o∾

Max was taken by a corporal to a barracks where he cleaned up and was issued a new uniform. He stood in the shower and slowly sunk to the floor where he began to sob.

He was overwhelmed by all that had happened and how powerless and useless he had been in the situation. He would spend day after day going over the scenario, having flashbacks, and blaming himself for the death of Bryan and his other mates.

⌘

On the sixth day after his narrow escape he was summoned back to headquarters where he met an American Five Star General. Even though he introduced himself Max couldn't recall his name.

"Private Johnson you may never realise how vital your reconnaissance of the Japanese staging camp was but I certainly do.

"After your return, we were able to find your comrades and bring them home, even that poor bugger Bignell who was decapitated.

"Among their things, we were surprised to find all the information gathered about the Japs. Why the hell they left this behind is anyone's guess. Possibly because they couldn't believe you found where they were.

"Anyway, all that information was vital in enabling us to catch the bastards off guard and to wipe them out. This has been a huge victory and one that will shorten the war. For your part in this heroic episode the United States of America thanks you profoundly.

"Neither America nor Australia can recognise your heroism on an official basis as you did not have a status for being in that area. Therefore, the Cross that should be bestowed upon you will be in memory only.

"I also am informed that the experience had brought on a severe case of Post Traumatic Syndrome so I am ordering you back to Australia and there you will be given a job training recruits in jungle warfare and getting them to see the rainforest in the same eyes that you do.

"Again, thank you." He saluted, clicked the little black case that he had in his hand shut, and marched out.

∽○∽

Max was given his orders that afternoon. He was to embark on a ship bound for Cairns in Queensland.

A camp had been set up 200 mile north of Cairns for the training of all Australian soldiers in jungle warfare. It was to be aligned with what Max considered to be important. All new recruits found it was a compulsory part of their training.

Training kids for jungle warfare was extremely difficult. Most had been brought up in city environments or open plain farms and so the oppressiveness of the environment and the high humidity took their tolls rapidly.

Max had been sent north of the Daintree to Cow Bay and there the army had a series of tents back from the highwater line.

He still had nightmares and shivered rough sweats as malaria had taken hold. Laying still for over hours in the mud, slush and rainforest had allowed all sorts of creepy crawlies to take advantage of his orifices and his warm blood.

The training program he had been able to develop was turning out crack jungle fighting men but too few of them. He would see 100 arrive all fresh and eager and then watch as day by day and night by night dozens would fall by the wayside.

∞∞∞

Luckily the war in the Pacific was taking a different turn and the allies were pushing the Japs back one island after another.

Max had heard it was Bougainville only last week so at this rate mainland Japan would soon be invaded.

Of course, the way these Jap soldiers operated, and Max had to assume the general population had a similar psyche, then a push into Japan would be suicidal by the allies as well as the Japs.

They rested everything on honour and were dedicated to the Emperor who they treated as their

God. They would rather commit hari-kari than surrender.

Max had even heard that the Jap fighter pilots were dive-bombing their zeroes onto the decks of warships and aircraft carriers trying to inflict as much damage as possible while committing suicide.

Max plugged on with the training giving every man a chance to learn all about the jungle and how to turn it into a friend and thus help you survive in the 6-week course.

∞

Late in 1945, he was sitting on the beach watching a huge saltwater crocodile wander by when a young lance-corporal came running flat out from the jungle.

He was the radio operator so Max knew something important was in the air. This kid normally did everything as slow as a turtle leaving the beach after laying its substantial number of eggs above high tide.

"Lance Corporal Gibbs whatever is the matter?" asked Max as the soldier came to a skidding halt.

"It's a bomb sir, a fucking great big bomb and we've dropped it."

"Whoa son calm down and explain who dropped the bomb and where. Sounds like another one of those fizzogs we keep hearing about in the Nevada Desert over in the good old US of A."

"No sir it was Japan and it was a place called Hiroshima. They said it was an atomic bomb dropped by a solitary bomber called the Enola Gay just a while ago this morning. They said it destroyed the city of thousands."

"Shit," spat Max, "That should stop the Japs in their tracks. Can't see them surrendering but if the Yanks have built a bomb that can take out a whole city, then it won't be too many more before there won't be a Japanese man, women or child left in the World."

"Come on we've got work to do." Max jumped up and ran off towards Snapper Island where he could see a number of recruits standing waist deep in water holding steadily to a dozen kayaks.

A few days later Max was standing in the radio tent waiting for the latest news or any fresh commands when over the crackling waves he heard of a second atomic bomb had been dropped on Nagasaki. "Bloody hell you'd think the silly bastards would throw in the towel. At this rate the whole country will be obliterated."

The voice of the Supreme Commander of the Pacific, General McArthur came booming out of the radio. "Japan must know by now that we have many more of these powerful atom bombs. They must know we will use them and destroy their country. They must know that the time for surrender is now. The emperor must step forward and offer his hand in unconditional surrender. He cannot wait any longer."

For Max the war ended that very morning when a gunboat appeared off the coast and a small rubber zodiac was lowered and came roaring up on to the sand.

The smart young naval lieutenant jumped on to the sand and saluted. "Private Johnson you are to wrap up this operation and then we'll get your men to Brisbane for demob. You will be pleased to know Japan has surrendered and the war is finally over."

Behind him Max heard a long whoop and fifty slouch hats went flying into the air.

Wrapping up a jungle training camp is not that easy. There were platoons operating in a number of areas that were not able to be contacted.

The rule was to maintain radio silence for the time the platoon was in the jungle.

There were tons of equipment that for whatever the reason was to be packed and carted to Cairns. To Max it would have been quicker and easier to simply burn the lot as it was never likely to be used ever again.

Max need not have worried as he was taken off the area by ship and sent south to be demobbed. He was lined up in a hall along with hundreds of others and required to fill in several forms.

∞o∞

One was to sever ties with the Army which was the discharge. Another was a questionnaire to determine his experiences over the time he was in the army. The final one and the best one was an account of money earned and days spent in different theatres.

Max's indicated he'd been in the Army in Australia for 250 days and in New Guinea for 27 days. His pay amounted to £446 and 65 pence. That was a princely amount.

∞o∞

Max visited home to tell his mother that he was going off on a holiday but would be back in a month or so. He had to get away from the old and learn what the new era was going to be like.

He headed for the bright lights of Sydney. He had heard about it many times and always wanted to visit and explore the most populated of all Australia's cities.

He caught the train and found a comfortable seat for the long journey. There were few people on the train in Cairns but the further south he travelled the more the passenger list grew.

The east coast of Queensland was beginning to be settled by people from all over Australia and overseas. The war had made it accessible to many nationalities and these people had passed the word to others from their country.

The train chugged along through Townsville, Mackay, Rockhampton, Bundaberg, Brisbane and the South Coast (became Gold Coast later on). The train continued its journey south through New South Wales and its towns Coffs Harbour, Port Macquarie, Newcastle and then Sydney.

The most valuable part of the time spent in Sydney was befriending Allan Groves. They met in the bar of the Castaway Hotel near Woolloomooloo and talked for hours.

It turned out that Allan owned a road paving company called Tar and Cement Repair Co. He was searching for workers who had the skills to drive trucks, rollers and graders.

He wanted those who knew how to mix hot bitumen and lay the right thickness. They needed to be efficient workers. He kept emphasising that workers of the calibre he was searching for was few and far between. For the right man he would pay wage one and a half times that offered by other companies.

It was certainly an incentive and one that Max would consider but the reality was he needed a rest not only physically but mentally as well. After the experiences he had gone through and the treatment he saw Bryan go through with the final episode being the lad's death he just wanted time to himself.

The pay was substantial and there was a lot of work in isolated places so being single was an advantage.

Max was happy to hear Allan's discourse about laying bitumen but at that point in time he just wanted to rest and take in the sights.

Chapter 14

Allan suggested to Max that if he ever needed a job, he would keep one open for him. All he had to do was call in at the workshop in Penrith and tell the secretary at the front desk that, "Allan sent for me to boost the company's profits." He laughed a deep belly laugh at his own humour. "That will let her know you are the special worker I have been waiting for."

The pay was substantial but there was a lot of work in isolated places so being single was an advantage.

Max was happy to hear Allan's discourse about laying bitumen but at that point in time he just wanted to rest and take in the sights.

As a tourist he trudged all over Sydney taking in the sights he vaguely remembered people talking about.

Of course, the 'Coat Hanger' or Sydney Harbour Bridge was not whispered about as it was a colossal bridge that linked north shore with the inner city and south Sydney.

It must have been a sight during the opening ceremony held on 19th March, 1932 as thousands packed both sides to see the tape cut by the Premier Jack Lang.

It must have been an exciting time watching Francis Edward de Groot galloping on his horse to slice through the tape before Lang could perform the act.

He wandered around Circular Quay and watched the ferries taking and bringing the workers and sight-seers to central Sydney.

He fought his way through the thick throngs of the crowds in the city itself. He stood looking sky-wards to the top of the skyscrapers that seem to dis-appear into Heaven.

The American Navy was still evident around the massive harbour and in the streets.

Max walked up to the Rocks area because it had historical significance. This was where the first white people settled when they arrived with captain Phillip back in 1788. The local indigenous people had been shocked to see the foreign ships arrive and considered that their land was being invaded. This thinking has been a sticking point in Australian history ever since.

Max went back to Queensland and started work on the dairy farm with his father. He soon discovered that his reputation preceded himself and with Keith chasing every girl in the district he became popular.

He was constantly being asked out to dances and being called out by local farmers to use his mechanical knowledge to fix this machine or that motor.

Although he was not one to big note himself it was rather disappointing that no one knew of his war time exploits. He worked hard to build up a warrior type persona and the men who saw him in action were always amazed.

∽o∾

One morning Max woke up and looked out the window. Half a dozen cows were munching grass and moving slowly. He thought, "Those cows are like me, alive but going nowhere. Just like me they keep repeating the same thing over and over. I need to get out and find other activities and people to mix with."

He climbed out of bed and dressed. He came into the kitchen where Marion was cooking bacon, eggs and toast in readiness for Max. The aroma and the way his mother fried the eggs so that the yolks were still runny was mouthwatering. He couldn't refuse the breakfast so he sat and ate.

He cut the toast into soldiers and dipped each, one at a time, into the bright yellow of the runny yolk. He placed the soldier with the yolk dribbling from the soldier into his mouth and savoured the yellow liquid as it brushed past his taste buds.

When he was finished, he stood up and announced, "I'm riding around Queensland to see all the sights. I shall return one day in the future."

Marion nodded her head. She knew he was still bothered by the demons from the war. It would take many years for him to return to his old self, if ever. She didn't protest but hugged him and said, "You enjoy yourself you deserve it."

Burton wasn't so forgiving and made a disparaging comment. "He needs to get on with helping around the dairy instead of leaving me with the whole burden."

∾o∾

Max had travelled light and fast and was now approaching the border, that imaginary line between Queensland and New South Wales.

The road he had been on was bush bashed, single lane, muddy and rutted. It wound through heavy rainforest and through mountains that made up the western side of the Great Dividing Range.

∾o∾

Riding the Triumph Tiger 100 had become an obsession ever since he had bought it outside the Tully Army Camp. It was a magnificent beast to ride and handled easily into the many twists and turns he found on his wanderings through Queensland.

There were major faults and he discovered them by accident.

One of his biker friends had warned him that paying a miserly £125 for a Triumph Tiger 100 meant the owner had either stolen it and was finding it too hot to keep or there was a mechanical problem. If it was the latter then Max needed to find and fix it or pay a hefty price in face and limb.

He rode the bike with one ear on the engine ready to pull up at any odd noise. This was his means to survival and so far it was working.

Max had a better than average knowledge of mechanics as he had been involved with motors since the age of eight when his father had rocked up to the Daintree dairy they owned driving a brand new Ford Tourer Pickup.

Old Burton had been smitten by motor cars since his early twenties. He had learnt to drive with his future brothers-in-law, the Stewart boys out on the selection in Bray's Creek.

There were 15 children in the Stewart family and all bar one had lived at Bray's Creek. Max's mother, Marion, was one of the older girls and a twin.

She and her sister Rose were the work horses of the domestic side of the household as well as spending hours riding their horses around the district to collect money for a new church in Tyalgum.

It was on one of these rides that she and Rose had come across Burton Johnson and she fell for the tall, handsome, red-headed Dane. Once she got him to visit, he was accepted by her family and she could begin courting him.

Four of Marion's brothers had arrived home in 1914 on furlough after answering the call to enlist.

Reuben had mooted the idea of pooling their money to buy a car so that they could learn to drive, give them more mobility and it would entice the local chics to join them.

The plan worked perfectly and Reuben was the happiest, carefree driver of them all. He liked nothing better than taking his turn at the wheel and chugging along at 20 miles an hour seeking out every water filled pothole so he could create a spray of water that would soak all and sundry. Even the pedestrians walking the streets of Tyalgum, Uki, Chillingham and Murwillumbah copped their drenching.

Burton joined the happy foursome as they drove around the district looking all dapper in either army uniforms or their best suits.

Reuben, working through a rotation list made sure everyone got a turn to drive.

Whenever they came to a halt there was great speculation as to what the problem was and how best to fix the mechanical monster to get the 'show back on the road'.

∽o∾

As the days passed it was Burton who began to prove he had the natural knack for diagnosing and fixing the mechanical problems. Marion, his wife to be, always had a gleam in her eyes when her brothers boasted of Burton's prowess.

Unfortunately, all good times and fun come to an end and the four Stewart brothers were called back to barracks and embarked for the Middle-east. Here they trained in modern day warfare, charging over trenches, bayonets fixed, into a wall of make-believe lead, shot from numerous machineguns while at the same time being desensitised to the constant screaming of 40-pound shells and then the deafening explosion as they hit the ground and blasted a nine-foot crater in the soft European soil.

Of course, all this was done under controlled conditions with blank ammunition and the explosions were kept well behind the rank and file that was charging up and down the hills.

War games ceased and the four Stewart boys were shipped out to various theatres of war from Gallipoli to Europe. Reuben, who had enjoyed his reckless but fun times on the farm splashing through the muddy potholes was sent to the front line in Pozieres in France.

The mud and slush was deep and widespread and the only way to move was along wooded footpaths.

The landscape which once boasted of pristine green fields and tall oaks was now a blasted desolate waste land. In a letter he had written back home to his mother Mary Jane he had tried to describe the indescribable and after many attempts finally wrote, 'The World has gone mad'.

∞o∞

He was ordered forward on one fateful day and was pressing quickly while watching mates around him being struck and killed by real bullets.

He heard his best mate call from his right and glanced across ready to lend assistance when he was stuck on the side of the face by a piece of shrapnel. It blew away half his face and he died instantly.

∞o∞

Burton stayed at home working the dairy for his father-in-law and was oblivious to the fate of his brother-in-law until he heard the wailing of Marion and her mother.

He ran to the house and saw the two arm in arm sitting on the kitchen floor. Marion held a telegram in her outstretched arm and he took it reluctantly and saw the dreaded words "Killed in Action" and then noted Reuben's name.

He bent gently and put an arm around Marion and stroked her back. What else was there to do?

Burton left the kitchen and wandered away from the house towards the barn, the same place Marion had seduced him two years ago.

∞०∞

Even with those sights meandering through his thoughts it was the car that stood out in the barn. There sitting proudly awaiting the soldier boys return was the Austin A40. He walked over to it, lifted the bonnet and began tinkling with the carburettor.

It was Max's dad who had introduced him to mechanics and just as well. He hated school and education so was pleased when the family left the Daintree in 1936 and moved to a dairy where it was not possible to attend a school.

Instead of the 3 Rs Max spent his spare time on the big M.

To add to his burgeoning mechanics knowledge his big brother Burt had bought a truck. This was ex-army and was forever breaking down. With uncanny skills Max could get it bursting back to life in no time at all.

Chapter 15

Burt added to his fleet and by the time the War broke out in 1939 he was running three trucks and had a car for the family. He hired Max to keep them all in tip top mechanical order.

Burt then discovered a more lucrative business although somewhat dangerous one. He added a bulldozer to his fleet and got Max to convert the trucks into semi-trailers ready for heavy haulage.

Burt now entered the timber industry. He had bulldozer drivers to fall the trees, a small mill to cut the logs and trucks to transport the timber to nearby mills.

Max was kept on as the number one mechanic and spent each day rushing from here to there as each machine dawdled to a stop for one reason or another.

In the meanwhile, Keith's libido was sailing full steam ahead and he was seeking out females at every opportunity. Often Max was strung along on these escapades but no matter how much giggling and touching went on he appeared not to be interested. He was there as his big brother's mate and that was all.

Keith had bought a model T ford and chugged around the district looking for easy pick-ups. As far as Max could fathom his efforts were successful but all of the girls simply used him like a taxi, promising much with their winks and quips but giving nothing in return.

One day they had run the ford along Moggill Road and took to the hill that led up to the chapel at the top. Keith had started the journey with three young girls in the car and of course Max sitting in the back between two of them. They had set off with the intention of going down to the Brisbane River for a swim.

The speed Keith had attained on the flat stretch of Moggill Road was just over 30mph so by the time they were half way up the steep incline he had run down through the gears and the car was coming to a halt. Keith called to his passengers to get out and push which they obligingly did.

With a lot of huffing and puffing and straining they managed to get the vehicle over the hump and it began to gather speed.

Max ran after the car, jumped on the running board and pleaded with Keith to pull up. After some 50 yards he agreed and the two fellows waited for the girls to catch up.

One of the women was angry and turned on Keith giving him a good tongue lashing. Another who was slim and blond went to Keith's aid, quietening her angry friend down and explaining on Keith's behalf why he had to ask them all to get out and push and why it took so long to pull over.

Keith was so impressed by this defence and the beauty of the young lady that he asked her name. She replied, "Laura. I'm Laura Pryde and one day I will let you ask me to marry you."

Keith smiled and said, "Well Laura Pryde I am mightily taken by your help and smitten by your forwardness. I hope we don't have to wait for Hell to freeze over for that proposal." Keith put the car into first gear and away they went on their journey to the river. As they got nearer they could make out the muddy look of the river a sure sign that it had rained heavily further north.

Max was frustrated with having to watch his big brothers take on responsibility for the war effort while he stayed at home and played silly games with his sisters.

He was only 16 and too young to contemplate joining up. He had even heard of kids as young as 15 going off to the recruiting office. Some snuck through and others were found out and sent packing home. Often a devastated mother would turn up at a barrack or at the wharf and demand their little Matty be sent home as he was still only a baby.

Max was keen to join up but Burton had impressed upon him almost daily that he would not sign any papers until the boy turned 18 and that was not until 4th June, 1944. He still had over two years to wait and no doubt by then the fighting would be over and peace would come.

"Hey dream baby come and play rounders," shouted Rita. She was always the one trying to keep everyone's spirits up and keep their minds and brains busy.

""We've pinched your tennis ball and set out the plates so if you don't care what happens to your precious ball then stay there," taunted Rita.

Max jumped up, tipped over the tin of oil he had so carefully balanced on the back wheel, cursed and ran flat tac after Rita. "You conniving little bitch, you wait until I catch you."

Chapter 16

Rita laughed and surged towards the open paddock. Ahead she could see Molly, Phyllis and Marge all waiting for the fifth player. As the two raced along the other girls were in awe of how Rita could always get her way.

"I'm batting," said Max as he pulled up at home base and grabbed the piece of wood that their father had fashioned into a baseball styled bat. He was still handy with the wood plane and the spokeshave.

"It's my tennis ball so I should be able to choose my team first." Like all the Johnson kids you didn't get much that you could call your own but once you did it became a precious possession. No one was allowed to have it unless express permission was obtained and that a fair deal was made. The object had to be returned in mint condition or compensation called for.

The tennis ball was Max's precious object and he was the only one in the family to have one. Without the ball no games could be played whether it be rounders, cricket or tennis.

Max got his way and chose Rita as the other team member. She was the fastest of the girls and had a good hard slog on her that would guarantee second base if not further before the ball was gathered by the fielders.

In rounders you had to hit the ball and run the bases in order while the fielders threw the ball to each base in turn, first, second, third and then home. If the runner beats the ball to home the team scored a run. If the ball beat the runner to home they were out and could no longer bat in that innings.

It was a fast, skilful and fun game although with the Johnson mob it could become extremely competitive and full of arguments about rules and who was in and who was out.

Today's game was more ferocious than usual and each team edged ahead of the other as the innings came and went.

At the back of the house and just a fence over from the paddock the family was playing rounders in stood the long drop. This was the loo, toilet, dunny, shithouse and any other name that may be used. It was a rickety wooden structure with a corrugated iron roof. At the back Burton had dug a deep hole of about four feet and round with a diameter of two feet.

When one needed to go and have a crap or a number two or a plain old hit they squatted across this hole and allowed the faeces to plop to the bottom. Once the hole became nearly full or someone complained of the overbearing stench, Burton would cover it over, move the structure further afield and dig another deep, round hole.

The present dunny was about half full so had a few more weeks use left in it. At the moment the family was playing their rounders game it stood like a sentinel on a slight rise with the door fully open. The opening was facing the playing diamond.

Molly was next up and was determined to put her team ahead as the teams were currently neck and neck. She hefted the bat and had two practice swings before crouching ready. Rita threw a slow curving ball that started high and dipped away. Molly was ready and hit it flush in the sweet part of the bat. The ball cleared the fence, bounced three times and headed for the open door of the dunny.

Molly was intent on running the bases so she didn't see where the ball went. Max was furious with Rita for such weak pitching but he now had to head the ball off and get it back to the bases to run Molly out.

He cleared the fence in a scissor high jump action and galloped along the line that he thought the ball had taken. Nothing appeared so he ran on straight at the door of the dunny. He looked around the outside and then inside, nothing.

"Oh shit," he yelled, "I think it's at the bottom of the long drop." He held his nose and bent over the hole and peered down. Sure enough, about two and a half feet down he could see the white ball stuck in the brown putrid muck.

Max came storming out of the dunny cursing and yelling. "You bastards have to get my ball back or I'll stick you all down there and cover each with dirt."

He set off to the nearby barn and returned with an assortment of ropes, bamboo sticks, binder twine, wire and a shovel.

By this time the game had ceased and the girls were gathered at a discrete distance from the dunny awaiting Max and wondering what his grand plan was to retrieve the ball.

"Right," he said, "One of you has to go down and fetch the ball. Either volunteer or be volunteered."

They all looked at each other but no one moved or offered. "Get hold of Marge she's the littlest and we'll tie her to the rope and she can reach down. If Rita and Phyllis help me hold the rope she won't fall in."

Marge went a sickly white with fear and the feeling of claustrophobia swept over her but she had to be brave or else Max would just toss her in. The ropes were tied around her waist and with all hands holding on they encouraged Marge to reach into the hole for the ball. "I can't reach deep enough and I can't see the ball as the hole is too dark.

Max was all the while trying to come up with a better plan. "The only way is to lower her head first, with her arms outstretched then she can reach far enough and with her head down the hole she should be able to see. We can control how deep she is lowered by tying on the bamboo rods.

They hauled Marge back out and set about tying the bamboo rods with the rope across her hips. The two pieces of wood allowed Max, Molly, Rita and Phyllis to hold one end each and lower Marge head first into the cesspool.

The elaborate frame was assembled and Marge given the instructions to hold her arms above her head. Next, she had to bend over the hole with her arms inside and her head pressing on the sides.

"Lift," said Max and the poles were lifted just enough for Marge to feel her feet come off the ground and then she flipped upside down and slipped into the hole.

"Hold her up, hold her up," yelled Max as he saw the diminutive figure start to disappear into the hole. All four bearers held tight and the body stopped descending.

"Can you see the ball and reach it?" asked Max.

A muffled, frightened voice could barely be heard from Marge. "I can nearly touch it but it stinks real awful down here. Get me out before I spew up."Lower the poles a few inches. You get the ball or we'll leave you in there for good. Grab and yell and we'll heave you out," said Max.

All the other girls were silent and hoping that they could extricate their little sister as easily as Max was making it sound.

"We drop her down it can't be too far," said Max.

"Got it!" came a triumphant shout and all the four bearers looked around and grinned. They set about hauling the little body out of the hole. Unfortunately the coordination that had been evident a few seconds ago got out of sync with Rita trying to haul faster than the other two girls and Max had let go in his desperate effort to get the ball that Marge was trying to pass backhand up through the hole.

Marge went crashing back into the dunny.

Chapter 17

Amid screams, curses and sheer fear she was grabbed by the feet by Max and pulled out. She was saturated and smelling to the high heavens.

Max gave Molly the order to get Marge washed up and covered with sweet smelling powder. He sent the twins off to wash the clothes and hang them out.

Max took upon himself to wrap his precious ball in newspaper and carry it to the bathroom where he washed and washed the ball until it was clean and smelling like roses.

∞∞

It was some days later that the girls were able to see the funny side of the whole episode although Marge would never recover from her soaking.

In fact Marge met with a different fate that had no direct relationship to her dunny experience.

∞∞

After his bout of home sickness, Keith returned to the Tully Army Camp and settled in. He was determined to be the best soldier the army could make him. This meant many days on parade grounds marching and carrying out drills and formations. It meant many nights and days on bivouacs where pitching a tent and sleeping under the stars became a part of life. It meant learning all about the rifles and submachine guns that you were issued with and had to strip, oil and rebuild in under 20 seconds. It meant learning the constellations of the stars in case you became disoriented and needed to find your way home. It was all about using a bayonet attached to your rifle and charging a chaff bag full of straw and jabbing the sharp knife up to the handle all the while pretending it was an enemy soldier not a wheatbag. Most of all it was being dehumanised so that you could dispense of an enemy soldier without hesitation and guilt.

Keith had begun his army training in earnest and was one of the more proficient First Aiders in his platoon.

"That's the way Private, hold the head back and pinch the nose to stop air from escaping. Now open the mouth and force a few breaths in.

Remember this is the latest method to get air into the patient's lungs. As you see the chest rises as you breathe into their mouths. Now watch again as the chest rises then you know the air is getting to the lungs. Now get Myers to pump his fist onto the sternum in a regular beat to get the heart pumping. This ladies is how you do CPR and this ladies is a demonstration by two of the best."

Keith hated the way the Sergeant always belittled the new recruits by referring to them as females. Most of the women he knew were as strong as any man, could hold their own in a fight, could swear as well as any man could, down a schooner just as fast and were a damn sight smarter. He felt like telling the stupid bastard all of that but knew better so kept his silence.

"Right all dismissed. Go get cleaned up for dinner and lights out is at 2100 hours," bellowed the sergeant.

The platoon had been at CPR drill all afternoon and were pleased to be given a rest.

Back at Kenmore Keith's mother Marion was ready to dish up the rabbit stew to the family. Each of the children had wandered in and sat at their allotted places waiting for the last to arrive. Finally Max sat and all bowed their heads.

Marion said grace, "Thank you Lord for the food that we are about to partake. Thank you for looking after us all and please keep an eye on Keith as he is in the army. Amen."

All the others repeated the "Amen" and then Rita cheekily said, "Two, four, six, eight, bog in and don't hesitate!"
Burton, her father, gave her a backhander across the face that sent her spinning out of the chair. She

looked up and held back the tears. "Don't you dare be so rude when your mother is talking to her God. Now sit up and eat your food."

Rita clambered back onto the chair and waited for Marion to spoon a ladle of stew onto her plate. She said a quiet, polite, "Thank you mamma." She looked over at Marge who was sitting opposite and asked, "Marge may I have a slice of bread, please?"

Marge was looking directly at Rita but did not move. She seemed to be frozen and her eyes were unseeing. Rita repeated the request with an emphasis on please then added, "Pretty please."

"You going to be smart again miss and you'll cop a second back hander," warned Burton. Rita stayed silent but couldn't understand why Marge was still unmoving.

Suddenly Marge threw up all over the table and she flopped to one side. As Marion stood to save her youngest child from landing on the floor, Marge began to convulse. She kicked back and forth and gurgled in her throat. The convulsions increased in intensity and Burton had to push his way to her and hold her down for fear she would do herself harm.

As the convulsing slowed due to Burton's efforts, Marge began to choke and stopped breathing. Burton took her by the shoulders and shook the limp little body. Marge responded by vomiting and then letting out a long breath. Her actions slowed and she fell into unconsciousness.

Burton picked her up and followed Marion into the main bedroom where they put Marge to rest. Eva was sent off to fetch the locum at all haste.

The elderly doctor diagnosed epilepsy and suggested that Marge be kept in bed and resting for at least a week to regain her strength and to see if the affliction would return. He recommended that any future fits be treated with caution. A piece of round wood like a half a foot of a broom handle was to be kept handy and jammed between the teeth at the slightest sight of a fit.

This was to keep the mouth open to allow breathing and to keep the teeth apart so that Marge did not bite off her own tongue or any part of a helper's anatomy. She was to be restrained as best as could be until the fit passed.

Marge had several such convulsions over the next two months. Some were mild and she settled quickly, others raged on and on and at times it appeared they would never stop until she became comatose.

One lovely, fine afternoon in September Marge had a massive fit and after nearly two hours of tossing and screaming out she collapsed and remained rigid. To Marion this was a different fit to all the others she had seen and in her caring way sent Eva and Isobel for the doctor.

A young man appeared with the girls and stated that he was the new district doctor. He introduced himself as Dr Bignell and set about examining Marge. He took his stethoscope to listen to her heart beat and her breathing. He checked out the mouth for any biting and looked down her throat for obstructions. He was gentle and concerned and kept shaking his head ever so slightly.

Dr Bignell took out a pencil shaped object that to the surprise of Marion proved to be a torch. He held Marge's left eye open and flicked the torchlight back and forth. He did the same to the right eye and then announced, "I will send for an ambulance as this young lady needs to be in a hospital. I will have her sent through to Brisbane Memorial and I will ride with her. I suggest Mrs Johnson that you pack an overnight bag and accompany us in the front of the ambulance."

"What do you think the matter is, doctor?" asked Marion with some hesitancy.

"That I can't say from my examination but it is certainly more serious than epilepsy. Once we get your little one to the hospital we can perform some specialist checks and have a number of very professional doctors give a better diagnosis."

❦

The ambulance arrived at the Emergency entrance to Brisbane Memorial Hospital at twenty minutes after seven and by eight o'clock a number of tests had been performed and numerous specialists and nurses had prodded and poked Marge's unconscious body.

Dr Bignell and another tall thin doctor motioned to Marion to step outside of the emergency theatre where Marge lay under an oxygen tent.

"The news is rather grave Mrs Johnson. Your daughter has had a massive stroke and we need you to prepare for the worst. We are all of the opinion that she will not last through the night."

Marion grasped her breast and slid slowly to the floor and began to pray asking God to help her and to send the Healing Angels to help Marge.

The two doctors motioned to a matron nearby and a quick, quiet conversation resulted in Marion being assisted to rise and be helped back into the emergency theatre. Here a chair was brought in for her to sit in and she shuffled it close to the bed and held Marge's tiny, pale hand. It was so cold it felt as though death had already taken over.

Marion began to pray and she spent the night drifting in and out of sleep and praying to God for all the help He could muster.

∽∽

In the morning four nurses and two orderlies arrived and moved Marge to a general ward. She had survived the night and this in itself had confounded the doctors.

The new bed had curtains draped around it so this gave some privacy but Marion could hear all that was going on with the other patients. She was too focused to let any distractions bother her and she continued to sleep, wake and pray.

The nurses were especially kind by bringing in food and drinks for Marion. They wet hand towels and showed Marion how to dampen Marge's lips and dribble small amounts of water into her mouth. They showed her how to roll the child so that she didn't get bedsores nor end up in a position that would cut off her breathing.

The other members of the family made efforts to visit but work on the farm had to go on and the long distance was a limiting factor.

Those that did manage to arrive at the bedside were so shocked and traumatised by what they saw of their once vibrant and clever sister that they vowed never to return.

All the talk around the dinner table was that they would prepare for the worst and bury their sister up at the cemetery behind the church on Chapel Hill.

∞

Keith was shocked when he heard what had happened to his favourite sister. They were ten years apart in age but something clicked between them from the time Marion brought the chubby baby home from the Mossman Hospital way back in 1934. She had been born on 28th December, 1933 but Marion stayed the regulation week in hospital before taking the ferry back up the Daintree River to the family dairy farm.

Keith loved her and the way she giggled at everything and anything. As she grew she was his constant shadow.

She was broken hearted when he announced he was signing up to go in the army. She couldn't believe he would leave her alone and she spent hours begging him to change his mind.

Now he had heard the news that Marge was in Brisbane hospital dying from a massive stroke and he was stuck in the barracks with no way to leave.

All furloughs had been cancelled and that prick Lieutenant Forsythe had refused his request for compassionate leave.

At about 0200 in the morning a week after he had received the news about Marge, Keith plucked up the courage to thumb his nose at authority. He dressed in army uniform and snuck out of the barracks. He made for the back fence and climbed up the cyclone mesh and over the three strands of barbed wire at the top.

He balanced on the top strands of the barbs and jumped. He unfortunately did not have full purchase and his right leg slipped and one of the barbs bit deeply in before being dragged out by his falling weight.

It wasn't a major wound but it hurt like hell and bled profusely. It would need stitching but for now he tied his handkerchief around it, grabbed his slouch hat from where it landed and high tailed it towards the main road.

Chapter 18

Keith knew it would take him several days to carry out the plan he had in his head. First would be to hitch a ride with a kindly truckie or two which should get him close to Brisbane.

Once in the city confines, he would use shanks pony to find and visit the hospital. He had to see young Marge and hold her hand once more before she passed into Heaven.

He knew his chances were slim as she had all but been declared clinically dead by the doctors. Keeping out of sight of the Military Police or MPs as they were referred to should be reasonably easy, although his khaki uniform stood out.

He reached the main road and trotted along until he saw a truck bay and as good fortunes there was a double parked off to the side. As he neared the truck he could see it was a Mack and the double carried foodstuff for the towns of the outback.

Keith knocked gently on the cab window and a grumpy voice called out, "What the hell you doing mate I'm taking a kip. I've been on the road for 18 hours straight. Got a gun pointed at you so state your business or be off!"

Keith gave a shortened version of his plight leaving out the bit about being AWOL and hoped the truckie would buy the story.

"Get in I'm on my way back to Brissie shortly so your lucks holding."

Keith happily clambered up the two steps on the passenger side and opened the door. An over powering smell of stale tobacco and beer hit him and he had second thoughts.

This silly bugger is driving half sozzled and that might mean a serious accident. He felt he had to take his chances so he slipped into the seat and slammed the door.

The interior light of the cab came on and a huge, bald-headed man stuck out a hairy hand and said, "Jake the Snake at your service."

Keith shook Jake's hand vigorously, noting the numerous tattoos along the arms. There were more across the chest and a flying angel peeped out from the dark blue singlet that Jake was wearing. "Keith," he said trying to keep things nice and simple and not give too much more away.

"Run away to see your little sister in hospital have you?" Jake was already well ahead in the guessing game and Keith felt intimidated by the manner of the truckie.

"I didn't have any choice. The kid is dying and the bastard army won't give me compassionate leave or anything. What else could I do?"

"Don't worry matey I'll have you at the hospital by lunch time so sit back and enjoy the ride."

The huge engine fired into life as Jake turned the key. He crunched the gears searching for first, released the air brakes and accelerated laboriously forward. "Got a fair load on so it takes a while to pick up but once we're mobile she'll run like a charm."

Jake pinged through the gears finally reaching the tenth and they set off cruising at 50 mph.

As good as his word Jake put Keith right outside the entrance to the Brisbane Memorial Hospital at 1120 hours. "Had to detour a few miles, well like 50 miles but I'm a sucker for sob stories and yours beats the cake. All the best buddy and I hope and pray the little girl comes good."

Keith slammed the passenger door, waved vigorously and mouthed, "Thank you," as the truck bounced forward and then accelerated away.

Keith looked around and saw the entrance to the hospital. He made a direct line for the opening when his sixth sense made him detour to the left.

He reached the window and looked in. Sure enough two burley men in Military Police uniform sat in the lounge chairs looking towards a long desk where a young nurse in blue uniform was talking on a telephone.

Keith noted that both the cops had truncheons hanging from their belts and knew this was their favourite way to subdue their victims. He didn't feel like a bash over the head at that moment so he looked around searching for another way in.

He noticed two men dressed distinctly in the white laboratory coat of a doctor moving down an alley so he followed them. Halfway along the two men entered a door and it banged shut behind them.

Keith followed and when he got to the door hoped that it was not locked. It was. Now he had to think of another way to get past the MPs and then find the ward his sister was being kept in.

He thought of smashing the fire alarm glass that had to be somewhere out the front of the building. That would have all the people inside scurrying in all directions. He decided that it was too dangerous as there could be patients who if moved might end up being cut off from the emergency equipment that was keeping them alive.

He sunk to the ground, took off his slouch hat and brushed the back of his hand across his brow. He was sweating profusely mainly from the stress he was feeling but also because of the high humidity.

He sniffed a few times as mucus slipped through his nostrils and the sensation caused him to sneeze. He felt embarrassed when he felt the runny snot dribbling across his mouth.

Without thinking he reached down to where he had tied the handkerchief and undid it. He reached to his nose and blew vigorously before wiping the mess onto the material.

He pushed the handkerchief higher to his brow and wiped away more perspiration.

He returned the makeshift bandage to the wound on his leg noting that it was a deep cut and still bleeding freely. It definitely would need stitches.

Just as he was readying himself to rise and go back to the front of the hospital the door swung open and a portly lady dressed in a white uniform and wearing a white habit walked out.

She looked at Keith and put her hand over her mouth as though something had startled her. Keith put it down to his presence in such an isolated place. His position and posture must have made him appear to be one of those homeless people.

She set off up the street and the door began to swing back to its lock position. Keith threw a leg out and caught it inches from shutting. He edged across on his bottom and pulled the door fully open.

He was in.

Marion was sleeping fitfully as she had been for the past three months. She kept drifting in and out of weird dreams none of them made any sense.

When she was awake, she would check on Marge and chat to her about the family and the life on the dairy farm.

Marge did not respond she lay deathly still with her eyes taped shut. Her breathing was shallow and she was getting thinner and thinner. How she was holding out was a miracle and in Marion's mind it was through the will of God that she remained on Earth. To her He had a special mission for Marge and that would be played out in the not-too-distant future.

Marion returned to her chair that she had set up near the bed and took hold of Marge's pale hand. She settled back and began chatting sweet nothings when she felt the hairs on the nape of her neck rise. Her first thought was that a breeze was blowing through but the sensation grew stronger and she turned.

She let out a blood curdling scream and began yelling, "Oh no not you too, not my Keithy."

Marion was staring at her son who she thought was back at the Tully Army Barracks and couldn't possibly be standing in front of her unless he was a ghost. To add to her terror the figure had blood all over his nose and across his brow as though he had been shot.

Keith stepped forward to hug his mother but she recoiled and sent the chair flying over. "It's me mother, Keith, I've come to visit Marge."

"No, it can't be you God must have sent you along which means you are dead," wailed Marion from down beside the bed.

A nurse came hurrying through the curtains and stopped abruptly. She turned and fled calling loudly, "Doctor, come quick the girl is awake. She's awake, it's a miracle, come quick."

While all the pandemonium was taking place around Marge she had regained consciousness and could make out her mother's voice and her brother Keith's voice.

She tried to call to them but couldn't make any sound. Her vocal chords had not been used for so long they were frozen.

Keith was the next to discover that Marge was awake and trying to sit up. "Oh my God I can't believe this, Marge you are awake."

He rushed forward and hugged her to his chest. Marion slowly rose to her feet and began sobbing. "Praise to the Lord, thank you my God for answer-ing my prayers. You are a miracle maker, praise to the Lord."

She pressed into Keith and Marge and when the doctor came through the curtains he saw a truly wondrous sight. He shooed the mother and son away and carefully pulled the tape from each of Marge's eyes. He began asking her question then realised she could not speak. He told her to nod or shake her head as a means of communication.

The doctor was elated to find that Marge was able to function almost normally although as she gained strength over the next fortnight it was clear that the stroke had left her weak down one side and her speech would always be slurred.

∞o∞

Keith was attended to by the other medical staff and the blood on his face was cleaned away and stitches placed in his leg. They reported him to the MPs who rushed from the ground floor to arrest him. He couldn't have cared less that he would be fined £5 and shoved in the slammer for ten days.

His little sister had woken up after nearly four weeks in a coma and the doctors thought she would make a good recovery. What else could a brother wish for?

∞o∞

Marion's belief in God was strengthened and would never be broken for the rest of her life. Her dedication to her daughter had paid off and they were re-united once again and for that she had God and the Healing Angels to thank.

Keith was nabbed by the two Military policemen and bundled into the back of an army jeep. The largest of the two escorts sat beside him with a handcuff attached to himself and another to Keith.

The officers making up the Court Marshall took some pity on Keith when deciding his fate for insubordination.

He should have been given six months in the slammer and loss of pay for the same time. Instead, the General in charge read out "Private Johnson in consideration of the desperate situation you had found yourself in the sentence will be lighter. We cannot, however, allow our soldiers to traipse off anywhere they like at any time they choose. An example must be kept to maintain discipline. You will be sent to the Army prison for one month and fined 4 week's pay."

The whole episode quietened Keith and his subdued manner was noted by Burton and Marion when he was finally released from gaol. He was now talking of leaving the army and going off to help Bert. His older brother with his transport business. Unfortunately, he had to wait until the war ended as the army declined his release.

At least one good thing came out of Keith's sojourn. Laura Pryde heard about the miracle he had performed in awakening Marge from her coma. So smitten was she that she made a special trip to the Johnson house in Kenmore to ask Keith to marry him. He readily accepted the proposal.

Chapter 19

Keith asked Max to be his best man which surprised everyone as the fashion was to seek out your eldest brother to do the honour.

Laura had become friendly with the two older Johnson girls so it was obvious that she would seek out Eva to be her lady in waiting and Isobel was her bridesmaid. She would have liked Marge to be her flower girl but that was impossible. The question then became two or one of the young ones?

The solution was Laura's mother's idea when she said, "Which ever way you look at the situation some-one will miss out so instead of one disappointment why not ask the three girls to take on the important job?" Laura was pleased with the decision and when the girls were asked they squealed in delight.

The wedding date was set for three months later which made it a Saturday 12th June, 1948.

Laura spent a whole day discussing who to invite and writing invitations to those selected.

Each invitation card was written out and put in an envelope before a stamp was licked and attached.

The Chapel on the hill was chosen as the marriage place so Laura and Keith drove up there to speak to the priest. Father Brockman was pleased for the two youngsters and found that he had nothing happening on June 12th.

The reception would be held in the Johnson house and Marion agreed to be home to arrange the decorations and feed all the guests.

The wedding went off like clockwork and the newlyweds disappeared on their honeymoon.

ⵗⵗ

On the following Monday a strange car was noticed by Isobel and Eva as it turned into the Johnson dairy farm. They sensed something might be wrong so split up to alert the family.

Isobel ran to the dairy to tell her father and Max. Eva ran inside the house to tell Marion and the young girls.

Marion waited patiently for the car to come to a stop. She looked out the window but could not identify the driver nor the passenger. As she watched the two visitors get out of the car Burton, Isobel and Max arrived in a hurry.

"Who is it my love?" asked Burton addressing Marion.

"Don't know but the mature lady had a thunderous face so it may not be good news.

Max was shocked to see that the other person was a girl called Annette who he had taken out on two or three occasions. He said, "The young one is a girl

Keith and I have taken out a few times. She is called Annette and works in Brisbane in a lawyer's office as a secretary. I would assume the other lady is her mother."

By now the couple was knocking on the door. With Marion going to answer the knocking everyone else scattered and made themselves scarce but, in a position, where they would be able to hear the discussion.

Marion opened the door and the visitor began with a loud angry voice, "I'm here because one of your men has made my daughter pregnant and I want them to own up."

Marion kept her composure and started by welcoming the loud mouthed lady.

"Good afternoon I am Marion Johnson. It is nice to meet you, Mrs…. I'm sorry I must have missed your name and the name of this young lady." The casual calm approach threw Mrs Manson and she started again with less anger.

"I'm sorry Mrs Johnson how rude of me. I'm Mrs Manson and this is my daughter Annette. I need to speak to you and your husband if he is at home?"

Burton was proud of Marion's approach and the anger abated from Mrs Manson. "I'm coming my dear," he called and began to walk towards the lounge room, while Marion invited the guests inside.

"Whatever is the matter Mrs Manson you can be assured we will meet it head on with you. Please sit down and I'll get my older girls to make you and Annette a cup of tea and some cupcakes."

All the ears hidden around the other rooms in the house strained to hear what the problem was and how Marion and Burton would solve it.

"Now Mrs Manson tell us the purpose of your visit today."

"My daughter, Annette is pregnant and she tells me she went with one of your sons. I am shocked and angry that she did not heed my warning about going to bed with boys. However, she is prepared to accept her part in the sordid affair. What I need to know is which of your boys was involved and are they going to own up and marry my girl."

Burton took over the conversation saying, "We have one on a honeymoon and one running his business so I would doubt they were involved. Our youngest, Max, seems likely to be the culprit."

"Miss Annette, can you tell Mr and Mrs Johnson the story you told me this morning after we left the doctor's surgery?" demanded Mrs Manson.

Annette began to sob and between these she told the following story; "Keith and Max are my friends and friends of other girls. We go to the movies and dances. We all have used the back of Keith's car to make love in. I did it with both boys so I don't know which one is the father of my baby." She began to cry.

"There Mr and Mrs Johnson is the truth of what your boys have been up to so they must pay for their waywardness."

"We agree wholeheartedly Mrs Manson. As soon as we catch up with two fools we will determine which has impregnated your daughter and they will marry her. Are you happy with that Annette."

Mrs Manson broke in, "Of course she will be and this must not be delayed. I cannot have my daughter's name dragged through the mud by the locals and their gossip. Next Saturday or before if you please, and thank you for your time." At that Mrs Manson was out of her chair and bustling towards the car.

The car engine started as Annette ran to catch up and as she clambered in the car accelerated away.

"We have a problem within a problem, my dear," said Marion. There can only be one boy accused and I think he is more likely to be innocent."

"I don't care we will not have our good name dragged through the gossip mill and we agreed to fix the problem so he will just have to accept his parents' solution."

"I may as well drive my motorbike into a tree or off a cliff or take my gun and shoot myself," was Max's plaintiff cry.

Annette and Max Johnson were married in the Methodist Church in Brisbane the following Saturday. The young couple did not have a reception nor a honeymoon. They went back to a flat in south Brisbane where Annette had taken over the main bedroom. She had already decorated it out as a baby's room. Max went to bed in the second bedroom which was stark having only a single bed in it. His mind was working overtime as to what he would do.

He scraped up all the money he could, sold any worthy objects he owned, asked his father for a loan and received £55.

In the middle of the night, several days since the wedding, he pushed his motorbike along the street and down the hill before kick starting it. He quietly headed north vowing never to speak to his parents nor his siblings nor his wife ever again. He was going to vanish for ever.

He rode all night and into the next morning. He lit a small fire beside the road and fried two eggs and a piece of toast. He pulled the blanket over his head and went to sleep.

Upon wakening in the late afternoon, he started the bike and rode off towards Townsville. He asked around for jobs in the outback but was told his best way of getting such employment was to be on the ground in front of the boss.

He set off once more heading west to Charter Towers then Hughenden. He stopped in the centre of town took off his helmet and left it on the seat of the bike.

A nearby store was a co-operative selling every knick-knack and food item anyone might need. He asked about a hand line for fishing and hooks. The shopkeeper wanted to know where he was going fishing adding that the barramundi were biting around Normanton and would take a bunny fly readily.

Max was thankful for the advice and paid the £2/ 2/2p and left. He turned the bike around heading east until he saw the Normanton sign post. It was dark when he pulled into the park at Normanton and cut the engine. He had always been inquisitive about the Gulf of Carpentaria and the rivers. Now he was there and he would take his time with the exploring.

He would wander from place to place hoping to find kind people who would feed him and converse with him. He was pleasantly surprised at just how many such persons lived on the planet.

He was immensely lucky at Normanton as he met a fellow traveller who taught him the tricks of catching and barbequing barramundi. He was able to offer to locals and newcomers barbequed fish and fresh fish every evening. This enabled Max to amass quite a sum of money over the few months he stayed in the tropics.

He knew his luck would faulter at some stage but not in the first year of his travels. After several weeks at Normanton he decided to go south through Cloncurry, Kyuna and onto Winton. His whereabouts while staying at Normanton was not revealed as most of the people coming and going to the fishing village saw Max as one of the townspeople.

It wasn't until Constable Filmer of the Missing Person's Bureau was following up a lead mentioned by a farmer from Townsville that the penny dropped. Filmer had followed the roads out of Townsville asking at garages and eateries if anyone had seen a Triumph Tiger 100. His research on motorbikes had offered a possible break so he had taken the lead by looking for Triumph Tiger 100s. According to import records only 300 Triumph Tiger 100s were landed in Australia from England. Of these eight were sent to buyers in Queensland. Filmer decided to find all of these bikes and see where they would lead.

He had already been as far north to the Daintree River Crossing but heard nothing. The trip out to Hughenden was one of changing scenes as you wind your way up the thickly forested mountains then down to the flatter plains.

The further west the warmer the temperature. Filmer stopped at all the towns along the way until he found himself in Hughenden talking to Albert Logan, the owner and manager of the local Co-op. "Sure seen a couple of those beauties in the past year, one went west headed he told me to Broome in Western Australia. The other talked about Normanton and fishing. In fact I recall telling him to take a bunny fly with him to catch burras.

The bloke set off back towards the turn off but haven't heard whether he got to do any fishing or what happened to him."

At Normanton Filmer found every second person knew a fellow who rode a Triumph Tiger 100 and fished for burramandi and mud crabs. He was also told he had missed the Barbeque Man by a fortnight. He wasn't Max Johnson he called himself The Barbeque Man and that was that. No one actually heard him mention a real name. Any way if he did it would have been false as anyone hiding would not offer up their real name.

Constable Filmer had done well but opened a bigger can of worms. From Hughenden he had the choice of west to Three Ways then south to Adelaide or north to Katherine or Darwin. The next possibility is to turn south to Winton and all of the small towns all the way to the New South Wales border. Then again Max Johnson may have turned around and headed for Townsville from where he had come from. While he was contemplating his next move the post mistress came puffing along the main street of Hughenden calling, "Constable Filmer your boss wants you back in Brisbane." In her hand she brandished a telegram.

Constable Filmer arrived back in Brisbane and passed on his information. The boss was pleased with the constable's initiative. He also told Filmer to pass on the information to Burton Johnson the father of the missing man. Burton was intrigued by the latest report but very confused. "I was told he was dead, even buried his pieces in the local cemetery now you tell me he could be alive because you found a man riding a Triumph Tiger 100 and has been fishing at

Normanton. Keep me informed I'm not convinced my boy is dead."

Max wondered at times what anxiety he may have caused at home but he never found any news about his disappearance so he thought they didn't care. He was gone, good riddens to bad rubbish.

The thought was far, far away from what was really happening at the Johnson household. The other to and fro thought was the buzz in his head. He would go over and over his story so far. He added possible consequences that he may have left others with.

The accusations levelled at Max mounted daily to a point where he said to himself, "Enough is enough. I've got to get out of here before I go mad." In the middle of the night he tied his swag on to the pillion seat. He walked his Triumph Tiger 100 far from the flat he was sharing with his new wife Annette and kick started it. He mounted the machine. Where was he going was anyone's guess but he intended never to return. He wondered what Annette was thinking and doing. Sometimes they were positive thoughts others rather dark. He knew she would be hating him for running off and leaving her to have the baby without any support.

Other times he imagined her sitting and sobbing not out of grief but because her little trick didn't work as she envisioned. It was Max she liked more than Keith so she was pleased that she had her mother believing Max was the baby's father when in fact she knew one hundred percent he was not. She hoped that Max, kind and considerate Max would do as his parents decided and that he would marry Annette as ordered. Once married she thought he would be the loving kind husband she needed. All he did was sneak away into the night and disappear.

As for the family, several members became concerned that Max was missing. Max knew they would be very ubhappy and demand everyone seek him out. Their searches proved fruitless.

As he rode along on his motor bike his thoughts turned to each one's frantic efforts of their searching.

Burton Johnson, Max's father, went to the local Brisbane Police to report his son's disappearance. He had him listed as missing as there was no evidence to indicate otherwise. This thought proved accurate and Burton told the family what he had done in his efforts to find his youngest son.

The local policeman, a Constable Regan had politely suggested that the description of Max led him to believe the man had wandered off into a different life style.

Burton would have nothing of that and got to being rather forceful towards the constable.

After the sixth visit and over a period of three months Constable Regan had had enough and agreed to send a report to Brisbane where the Missing Persons' Bureau was a section inside the Queensland Police Department.

This is how Detective Sergeant Tom Doritich came to be placed in charge of the Johnson case 247JOH. With a small team he made exhaustive enquiries but nothing turned up.

The Detective-Sergeant was left in two minds after talking to the Johnson family and some of Max Johnson's mates. On the one hand he seemed to have been a strong man in mind and body with a bright future ahead.

On the other-hand the emotional turmoil that had followed him since being demobbed from the Army may have tipped him over the edge to do something stupid.

Dorotich found out about Max's life since being released from the Australian Army and at times it wasn't pleasant reading.

Max went home to Kenmore in 1945 and began helping his father on the dairy farm.

They did their jobs but stayed at arm's distance due to a number of issues and incidences between the two since 1935.

One issue was involving the old man giving Max a severe hiding using a lawyer cane because he believed the boy lied to him and his mother. The mother was also angry because Max was reported by his older brother, Keith, for blaspheming. Another concern for Max as told by his wife Annette, was that the father forced the youngster into boxing bouts with his older and stronger brother. He had been beaten many times.

The older brother, called Keith, appeared to get Max into trouble over a number of issues.

The most devastating of these was to do with Max being pressed into marrying Annette. The young girl visited the dairy on occasions and was friendly with some of the Johnson family.

Max vehemently denied having sex with this girl and went onto say he'd never had sex with any female. The father had wiped this comment off and told Max he had to maintain the family honour and marry the girl. Even though she knew the truth of this situation Annette had remained silent hoping such a marriage would be a win to her.

Detective Doritich sent out to all Queensland police stations a Missing Person's pamphlet asking to be notified if any news regarding Max was revealed. The information was flimsy and lacked in a quality description. This would create major problems for Doritich.

∽o∾

It was several months before the first possible sighting was lodged with the Missing Person's Bureau in Brisbane. Detective Sergeant Doritich wrote out the details and placed the sheet in a file entitled Johnson, Max.

Before putting the file in a cabinet in his office he called his team in to let them know what he had been told. The story had come from the police in Townsville who mentioned a local seeing and hearing a motorbike speeding past his property in the middle of the night. He had lived in the area for 50 years and never heard a motor bike driven so fast before. He had the feeling that the rider was running away from someone or something.

He felt he needed to report the strange happening as it may be linked up with other information that could help find the rider or even someone who was a missing person.

Doritich told his team that there were only 5 missing persons in Queensland that disappeared whilst riding a motor bike. He added that the rider of the Townsville bike had only three directions to continue to run or he might still be in the area.

∾

Max's muddled mind sifted through the stories that he constantly tossed around. Today he settled on the day he was told to marry Annette.

Max walked into the lounge room and sat down. "This is so unfair dad and you know it is. I am not the one involved, in fact to this day I have never been with a girl in a way that would make her pregnant."

"Too bad, you are the only one who can make this situation right. You will and I say that again, you will help put this right."

∾

Max slowly cleared his thoughts and found himself looking impressively with the farmlands on the way into the little town of Winton. The sheep flocks ranged high and low in numbers. They were merino bred and their fleeces were being sold for top pounds. The grasslands were extensive keeping the sheep in good condition.

Max was also surprised by the cars that the local farmers were driving. He passed several coming and going from the town. These included a Rover 75 sedan, a Studebaker, a Chrysler and a Dodge.

The Triumph Tiger 100 bubbled to a stop outside the garage that had the sign Johnson Motors emblazoned on it. He smiled to himself and wondered what their relationship might have been. At least he wasn't using that surname so they wouldn't query anything to do with his ancestry.

The drive way attendant came to Max who asked for the petrol tank to be topped up. He stared a conversation and told the young chap on the bowsers how impressed he was with the town and the farms. He got quite a shock at the answer. "You wouldn't believe this but two years ago we had a long, drawn-out drought. The farmers had to sell their flocks and many were ready to walk out. He told Max the cost of the petrol and suggested he book into the Central Hotel as it had air-conditioning.

Max thanked the lad and waved a cheery good-bye. He rode up Elderslie Street and pulled into the hotel. He thought about seeking work as it seemed that the farmers were throwing their money around as they tend to do after a good season. He decided to get a rest and head on tomorrow, he having heard that Longreach was a place worth staying at for few weeks.

Max awoke early and paid his bill, A quick dash up the highway would land him at Longreach. Alas the town was accurately named as it takes forever and a day to get to it.

Only one main road in and out and sheep stations surrounding the town.

Max pulled up at the hotel and booked a bed for the night. He had slept rough for most of his time at Normanton so a second day privilege wouldn't hurt

He sat in the bar with an icy cold schooner and sipped away He intended to make the drink last until closing time.

He had asked the barman about the possibility of work on the farms and he had said he'd keep an ear open.

It wasn't a surprise when Max was approached by a tall, sunburnt cowboy who was very direct. "You looking for me, sonny?"

"We are shearing 4000 sheep and need a rouseabout starts tomorrow 0600 hours but we are eighty miles west so you would need to get out there tonight. Drive towards Jundah and you will see the station sign post. It's called 'Beyond Beyond Sheep Station'. Over the cattle grid and the house and shearing shed are five miles in."

Max was pleased and said, "I'm your man, I'll be there," He spent 4 months with the shearing team and when they found out about his mechanics knowledge and skills they wanted to keep him on, "Sorry but I need to keep moving and four months is about all I can afford at any one stop."

Max pulled into Longreach to top up the fuel and get some supplies. A young lady of about sixteen came

out of the shop to attend to his needs. She had that Tomboy look with overalls head to toes, boots tied with laces and a scarf around her head to keep her brunette hair from getting dirty with the grease and oil that was around the garage. As usual Max was in a talkative mood and began to tell the girl how impressed he was with the surrounding countryside.

Martha, as she had introduced herself, said to Max, "You wouldn't believe this but two years ago we had a long drawn out drought. The farmers had to sell their flocks and many were ready to walk out.

The entire year's rainfall was 4.5 inches and most of this fell during a thunderstorm in summer. The farmers ploughed their paddocks and seeded them as they always do. They hoped the rain would come but nothing eventuated. In the end they opened the gates to the fields and allowed the sheep to graze the little grass that had germinated. It was the saddest sight anyone had to face."

Max was shocked by all this news and tried to imagine what stark paddocks that were just dust bowls must have been like.

He imagined the wind whipping up the loose sand into dust devils as the cock-eyed bobs were so aptly called by the farmers.

She also mentioned that the Cobb and Co used to deliver through Longreach. The original stagecoach still sat in the sheds behind the bakery and there was hope that one day it would be fully restored.

Max thanked the lady and waved a cheery good-bye. He rode up Eagle Street and pulled into the hotel. Inside it was cool and devoid of human habitation. Max called a number of times but still the silence pervaded. He noticed a small bell sitting on the reception desk and walked over to it. He pressed the lever at the top and a shrill noise echoed inside the bar area.

Heavy foot falls were heard moving swiftly from out past the swinging doors that led out of the bar area. A strong, loud voice called, "Okay keep your knickers on I'm coming."

Max was surprised when a female figure, aged in her fifties appeared moving swiftly considering the portly figure she had allowed herself to grow into. "You need a room or a beer?" the lady asked.

"Both," said Max and continued, "And if possible a job."

"And you are?" queried the lady.

"Apologies," said Max who was embarrassed by his poor manners. His mother would have been most upset at his lack of introduction. "My name is Max Jenkins on a working holiday around Queensland," replied Max.

"Room 45, beer is in front of you and you need to keep asking anyone you see about a job and that should soon be filled."

Chapter 20

Constable Filmer was becoming a bulldog in his endeavour to prove or disprove that Max Johnson was alive or dead. Like all bulldogs who are trained to hold on to a suspect and never let them go until commanded to do so, Filmer was ready to pounce and hang on. He had once again followed the tracks of a vagrant riding a Triumph Tiger 100. He had decided that Max would need money, food and petrol and these were more available to the west and south of Charters Towers.

Filmer had started in Townsville where a witness assured the policeman that a male riding a Triumph Tiger 100 had driven through a few weeks ago. He was adamant the bike was headed west. From the map he consulted daily Filmer could see a pattern between Charter Towers and Cloncurry. His growing theory was that Max Johnson was a nuclear family man and would try to stay in touch with his grandparents, parents and siblings. From his information and placing each household on the map he could see that the triangle between Townsville, Cloncurry and Toowoomba contained the most of these people. He would hunt on a line, south and north. Grandma Stewart was a person of interest as many of the Johnson children had spent time with her during family crises. She was Marion Johnson's mother and resided in the small town of Tyalgum in New South Wales.

Max was fond of the octogenarian so there is a possibility that he had cut back from Miles to Tyalgum. The small town was in the picturesque area of the Mount Warning and a stone throw over the New South Wales border is the township of Uki another place mentioned by his boss Detective Sergeant Doritich. He knew he would have to take bits of the areas as he still had other jobs to investigate.

Filmer pulled up at a garage, in his holden, that had the sign Johnson Motors emblazoned on it. He smiled to himself and thought that this was ironic.

The drive way attendant came across and Filmer asked for the petrol tank to be topped up, oil, water and the tyre pressures checked. He started a conversation and told the young lass of his quest. The youngster was able to tell Constable Filmer all about three fellows who would fit his description. One lived in town and he offered that man's address and gave directions to the house. The other two were just riding through, one going north, the other south.

Max had to dress with waterproofs on as it was drizzling with rain when he revved the engine and set off back to Longreach and then turn right at Barcaldine to get to Charleville. The distances were immense but he learnt to put his mind in neutral and his speed down to 60 mph and in no time you would reach your destination. From Charleville to Roma, onto Dalby before heading back to Brisbane to report to Detective Sergeant Doritich.

It wasn't too soon and the boss offered him a raise to take on being a mobile mechanic. This involved driving thousands of miles every week to help desperate farmers to get their engines fixed and working again. These men were so grateful to have someone who could solve their mechanical problems in a matter of hours and they could get on with shearing or other pursuits.

Max was on the road again heading south. He had many options presented to him on the sign posts as he rode by. Stanhope, Tamworth, Moree, Coonabarabran and Gilgandra.

A few months later a strange story was related to the Missing Persons Bureau that sent Detective Dorotich scurrying to the township of Numinbah.

It was technically out of his jurisdiction being just over the Queensland – New South Wales border.

When he reached the town he was met by a middle aged lady by the name of Daisy who had written what had happened from the first day that

Max J arrived on his Triumph Tiger 100 motor-cycle to the time he disappeared in the Mount Tambourine forest. She had been brutal in her retelling of the story.

"A young man rode into town on a Triumph Tiger 100 and stopped at the gates of the Tatton's Roadworks Company looking for a job. He said his name was Max James but none of us believed that but he was so confident and a good worker. The boss, Felax took him on.

"The caretaker was the first person he met; "What's ya name sonny boy?" asked the old fellow standing guard at the road work company gates.

"Max eh, Max James" replied the visitor. "I'm looking for a job and somewhere to bed down for the night. I've been on the road for three days."

"And where are you headed if I may ask?" queried the old bloke. He began to cough, a dry cough that one would easily identify belonged to a heavy smoker.

"Actually making my way slowly from Brisbane to Sydney town. Hope to reach the city lights next year about this time. Now what about a job, surely you can use a strong young fellow like myself."

"Young, yes," agreed the man but before he could add anything more a hulking six foot six inches of a man came around the corner of a nearby shack. "What's the kid want?"

Max was taken aback at the size of the new bloke and sucked in a deep breath. He was huge, ugly and mean.

"Kid wants a job Felax but I don't think we have one for the likes of him."

Felax strolled towards the pair and stopped short of steamrolling Max.

"Job aye and what can you do, frighten the rabbits away, sweep the floors like a woman, fix up an infernal steam roller that won't go? Which one?" Before Max could take a pick the two jokers started laughing and the monster called Felax said, "Get on yer bike buddy before I'll kick you up the Khyber."

Chapter 21

"Fix the steam roller," snapped Max ever so quickly because he saw it as the only chance of a word before this big hulk lays him unconscious.

Felax stopped short of beginning a belting to this kid called Max. "Fix a steamroller, bullshit. I've got 22 men on the pay roll and they've all had a go and still she sits in the back yard like a dead turtle. Can't make up my mind she's just slow like the turtle or dead like the turtle I ran over the other day." He went into a laughing fit and Charley coughed and laughed in unison."

"Fair dinkum," blurted out Max, "I can mend anything mechanical quick and easy."

"Okay you, smart arse I'll give you three days to get the thing working. After that we'll take you in town and give you to one of Daisy's girls and they can exhaust you before throwing the body on the rubbish heap."

Felax reached out with a huge hairy paw, grabbed Max by the collar, twisted it and then frog marched him towards the back of the buildings.

As he walked, he called, "Come on you lazy good for nothings, got a bit of sport, betting and a good belly laugh for all of you. Steam roller in 60 seconds to get the gist of my yelling."

Twenty men appeared miraculously from the buildings and one came running still tying up his trousers with binder twine. His zip was still open and he didn't wear under pants.

Felax let Max go, walked to a nearby tool box and lifted it with one hand before dropping it within inches of Max's toes. "You got 3 days kiddo get working."

Most of the onlookers chortled and turned and went back to their work. They'd seen Felax play this game with many a rookie over the years. It was bloody cruel and impossible to achieve.

Felax had doctored the old roller and had several parts hidden in his office. Without these the machine would never work unless....

Max walked around the huge steam roller checking that water, spark plugs, in the correct places and filled to the height of the dipstick for oil and petrol.

Next, he clambered up the steps and sat in the seat. He reached forward and turned the key that was in its correct place. The engine whirred and ceased.

He grinned from ear to ear and stepped down from the roller. He slid the bonnets off the engine fiddled with some parts, shook his head and said to Felax, "Can I have the carburettor, starter motor and gasket please as they are missing.

"I can fashion them out if you would prefer. A visit to the town dump will be the best bet."

Felax was about to do a Rumpelstiltskin when he burst out laughing. "Smart little bugger aren't you. I'll get your requested parts from me office. Anything else while I'm about that errand?"

"Yes," called Max. " I need a couple of gallons of diesel as I need to drain the petrol out of this diesel fuel tank and fill it up with the correct fuel."

The engine was ready within the hour and all the workers of Tatton's Roadworks Company came out to see what Felax was going to do now. If this kid gets the roller to work Felax may take it as a smart alec outdoing the boss. Then again, he may crown him as a clever dick who was worthy of a place on the team. Time would tell.

One thing all the workers learnt about Felax was that he was one jealous bugger and could be cruel beyond belief.

They wanted to warn the young fellow who everyone was now calling Max but knew better to keep quiet.

Max climbed to the top of the steps of the roller and disappeared into the interior. The door slammed shut and then the engine begun ticking over then fired into life. Max put it in forward and the huge machine moved steadily forward. He threw the gear into reverse and began travelling in the opposite direction to his initial one.

All the watching crowd were suitably impressed and clapped. The machine had sat dormant for over a year and had become a toy for Felax, was now in working condition.

Felax moved his hand across his throat in the signal to cut the motor. Max obeyed and then clambered down to the ground. "That deserves a beer or two. Come on lads the first round is on me."

The band of workers all set out together making towards the centre of the town. It was a small place with a hotel, cooperative shop, school, post office and three houses. The men headed directly for the pub.

Those walking closest to Max congratulated him and then whispered, "Watch out for the boss he can be unpredictable especially after a few beers or when any one shows an interest in his woman."

Max got the first part but was yet to follow who the woman was that they spoke of.

Everyone trooped into the hotel where a lone middle aged woman stood behind the bar. "Get everyone a schooner Daisy and put it on my tab," called Felax as he walked inside.

"Yes love," called back the barmaid who Felax had addressed as Daisy.

"Daisy," thought Max "This must be the woman Felax has been talking about. Seems nice enough but I don't see what Felax sees in her. Bit of a plain Jane if you ask me."

∾०∾

The time flashed by as it always does when you are drinking alcohol and yelling to others so they can hear you in a crowded bar of a hotel.

Felax sidled up to Max and said, "You must meet my Daisy kiddo and then we find you somewhere to board. You be my worker, my mechanic and roller driver, yes!"

"Sounds good to me," said Max as he followed Felax to the bar.

"Hey Daisy this is Max a new boy who is clever mechanic he works for me now and stays with you upstairs in the front room. Okay by you, my girl?"

∾०∾

Max settled into to the routine of working on the local roads and going back to the hotel where he boarded with Daisy and two other young ladies. He soon worked out what the three ladies got up to especially after closing time.

Felax was always on hand to check on the customers and to move them along if there was any impending misbehaviour. He also made sure the right money was handed over for the pleasure that was given.

∞

Max, Felax and Daisy became buddies and their bonding was such that they would go out into the woods to a small house to enjoy a weekend together or to go hunting in the thick forest or fishing in a nearby lake.

Felax was a keen marksman with a crossbow. He used steel bolts to shoot at the larger animals and could accurately hit his prey at 50 yards.

Daisy joined in all the fun and did the cooking for meals. To Max he was in heaven although he did notice that Felax kept Daisy with him wherever they went. At night the noise from the main bedroom was unbearable but thankfully short. No sooner had the grunting and moaning finished Felax would begin snoring. Max followed suit and got a full night's sleep.

∞

One evening the three friends were sitting on the verandah watching the sun slowly slip behind the horizon. Felax lit the hurricane lamps and turned up the lights. Daisy walked past Max and stopped and took his hand in her hand.

What's the ring on your finger?" she asked.

"Oh they are the initials of my name. My mother gave the ring to me one Christmas."

"What's the J stand for. You have always been sort of secretive about your surname."

Felax was staring at the two, one sitting and the other standing. It wasn't the posture that he was looking at but rather the way Daisy was holding Max's hand.

Felax jumped up and fired one word at Daisy. "Bed!"

Daisy dropped Max's hand and like an obedient puppy followed Felax into the bedroom.

Nothing more was said about the situation although the grunting was louder than usual that night, Felax slept soundly for 12 hours.

Max was concerned that the innocent touching between Max and Daisy may have tipped Felax near to the edge so he kept his distance and only spoke when spoken to by Felax.

It was several weeks later Max was awoken by light tapping on his door at the hotel. He struggled to wake himself into full consciousness. Upon opening the door Max was surprised his visitor was Daisy all still all in her eye catching working dress and face plastered with make-up. To Max it appeared she had just finished working and should have been with Felax on her way to her own room.

Daisy was fidgeting and she looked like someone on a mission where the message was the vital part of the visit. "Hello Max, sorry to wake you but I have an invite from Felax telling you he wants you to be at the at the cabin for a weekend of hunting.

The words tumbled from Daisy before she turned abruptly and walked swiftly down the corridor. Max stood still and watched the receding figure of the wholesome Daisy.

Max settled back in bed and his mind began calculated what the real message was all about. For Daisy to be seeking out workers at four in the morning was unheard of, her fidgeting told him she was being co-erst and in fact didn't want to deliver any such message. The message appeared to be normal so why the shaking hand and the flicking eyes away from his? The haste with which the message was delivered and in a loud voice had warning bells all over it. Clearly Daisy was under duress to speak loud enough for a third party to hear it. Something was afoot and Max, for all his training, could not place his finger on it. A weekend hunting in the forest with Felax would normally be enjoyable so why did he toss and turn for the next four hours?

Chapter 22

Max felt reluctant to accept but Daisy had left too abruptly for him to accept or reject the invitation. Why was he still unsure that he should go hunting? Finally he decided that the best of the two evils was to accept the invitation. Daisy's message had indicated that she and Felax were going up to the cabin on Friday night and he should come along early, Saturday morning.

Max waited out the three days and early Saturday set off for the cabin. Upon arriving Max was concerned to see Daisy waiting on the verandah in a short dress and see through blouse. Looking at her took Max's breath away but he fought to control his emotions. "Where's Felax?" questioned Max.

"Oh he'll be along later this afternoon. He had a business deal to attend to," said Daisy.

There was a huskiness in her voice and Max began to hear in his head, "Warning, warning."

"Come on in and I'll make a cuppa and offer you some scones I made last night."

Daisy walked inside and Max, reluctantly followed. Daisy busied herself making a cup of white tea with two sugars. She cut two scones in half, buttered both pieces, added plum jam with a dollop of cream on top of each. She served these and wandered off towards the bedroom.

Max sat at the table and enjoyed the scones and the tea.

All the while he agonised over whether to get up and take off back to town.

He kept thinking that if Felax could throw a wobbly because his woman held Max's hand innocently what would he make of Max being alone with his sheila?

Daisy had been gone some time and Max was worried stiff so he stood up to make for the door when he heard Daisy say, "Come on big boy I'm all yours for the rest of the weekend. Felax doesn't know I'm up here and I'm sure you didn't tell him you were coming this way."

Max nearly ran but something stopped him. It wasn't every day that a woman like Daisy would be keen to get into his trousers.

Daisy took the lead and walked up to Max and led him to the bedroom. Max thought he had to be in a dream. He could not wake himself up and went quietly along.

Daisy lifted his hand to her lips and kissed each knuckle. When she reached the knuckle of his ring finger she stopped and said, "What's the ring for? You never did tell me."

He laughed and replied, "No such luck. My mother gave all of us a signet ring in case when we reached Heaven Saint Peter would not recognise any of the family. Mother was very religious and also at times illogical. We all cherish our rings."

Daisy said, "Oh how sweet, may I wear it while we are together?" She twisted at the ring and it slid easily from his finger. She placed it on her own ring finger and quietly said, "M J what does that stand for?"

"The initials of my name, Max Jefferies."

'Now I can be Moana Jefferies if you are gentle."

Max laughed and fell on to the bed with Daisy pinned gently beneath him.

A few hours later he awoke to find Daisy was missing. The whole plan was her idea and he fell for it, hook, line and sinker. He was certainly losing his ability to determine if people were up to no good or not.

Then he heard cups and saucers touching and making a pinging sound. She was in the kitchen making a cup of tea. He found his clothes and hurriedly dressed. He made the bed as immaculately as he knew how, making sure there were no evidence left behind. Just one pubic hair that wasn't blond and he was dead meat.

Max walked into the kitchen and said to Daisy, "I've got to get the hell out of here and now. When Felax discovers that I have been in bed with you he will stop at nothing in killing me."

Daisy turned to him and walked up close. "There were only the two of us so how will he know. You did enjoy yourself didn't you. I definitely did."

"Sorry Daisy but we need to get out of here and fast. I'll take the car back into town and bring the Triumph Tiger 100 back to pick you up. That will take no less than 30 minutes so get yourself ready."

"I can't go with you Max. Please stay I promise you Felax will not find out."

"Sorry Daisy but I need to get both of us out of here well away from Felax. I'll be back in 30 minutes. Travel light."

He dropped the car that belonged to Daisy behind the pub in the usual place she leaves it and sprinted upstairs, He grabbed a few belongings and ran down the back stairs.

His Triumph Tiger 100 was parked inside the company fence so he had no choice but to sacrifice it. The hike back to the cabin would take three hours at the double.

∽∘∽

Luckily he had come around the corner of the little cabin quietly or things would have turned out ugly. It had become a habit of Max's to whistle his favourite tunes when he was in a happy mood and lately this was most of the time. This time he was too deep in thought to be whistling.

The way that Daisy had overwhelmed him yesterday had shocked him but excited him in such a way that he was confused. He wasn't ready for a woman in his life nevertheless a full-on relationship. One girl can't have two men. This was a recipe for major TROUBLE.

He crept to the end of the side wall where there was a 44 gallon drum positioned to catch the overflow of rain from the roof. This then supplied drinking water to the house. There was a drum on each corner giving 176 gallons to see out any dry spell.

Up here in the mountains it was rare to have even one day when some precipitation didn't fall so that amount of water was more than sufficient.

His sixth sense, honed in the rainforest of the Daintree as a kid, was screaming at him, "Warning."

He ducked down onto his haunches and peered around trying to catch a 360-degree view of his surroundings. His forward scout skills came flooding back to him and then he saw Daisy.

"Oh my God what has he done to her?" he thought to himself as he saw the unconscious figure of the woman, bound by a thick rope to a tree some 60 yards away. Her curly blond hair flopped over her pale white face and the rope was wrapped around her neck, between her ample breasts and wound several times across her legs. She had a piece of black duct tape stuck over her mouth.

Max's kind side told him to run to her and untie the ropes and rescue her from the pain. He knew better and could see that she was set up as a decoy to catch the unexpected in a trap, one that they would not come out of alive.

Chapter 23

Max carefully peered over the rim of the 44 gallon drum. The water was brimming to overflowing and he wet his nose trying to get into a position to see what was happening on the verandah.

It was here that all the action was taking place. Felax, the huge Slav that he called a mate, sat in a chair holding onto a cross bow. He kept pulling the thick elastic sling back and forward using his right knee to assist.

Over the back of the chair, he was seated on was a quiver held in place with a leather strap. There were about ten steel bolts sticking out. Max could make out the notch that had been filed into the top of each and surmised that the other end was ground down to a sharp point. These were the bolts for the crossbow, Felax's favourite hunting weapon. "Silent, ever so silent but deadly," he would say and run his huge hands all over the bow.

On the table directly in front of him was a double-edged hunting knife. It was the one used to slice off the head of the wild pigs and rip open their guts. Felax was at his best when he was butchering the pigs or any of the animals they killed and ate.

He had a grin across his face and was humming quietly a tune in Yugoslavian. Max didn't know the words but they obviously pleased the ex-commando.

A heavy 303 rifle lay on the far side of the table and Max could make out a clip. Was there any ammunition in the gun? Then there was the problem of getting to it.

He ran through his options searching for the strengths of each and worrying about their weaknesses. Somehow, he had to try to save Daisy and, in the attempt, either kill Felax or be killed.

First option was the easiest. The army impressed constantly to look out for number one. In other words keep yourself alive and come back and fight another day. He dismissed this notion instantly as he ached all over for the situation, he could see Daisy was in. She must have gone through hell but what had triggered such a violent and senseless reaction?

The second idea was to take out his pocket knife that was in his trouser pocket. He carried it everywhere and it was handy.

He knew that a man with Felax's stature would hardly feel the blade and it would more than likely snap off leaving Max defenceless. The huge Slav weighed in at 240 pound and was trained finely in unarmed combat.

Even when they were fooling around Felax could swing Max up and over his shoulder and wander off with him in what he called the 'Fireman's Lift'. Max always felt so vulnerable and swore never to get in close to this man if the going got tough.

The going was now tough.

The coward's action was to turn tail, sneak away and never return. This could be accomplished with little noise as he would high tail it by foot.

Felax had obviously not twigged that Max was sitting barely 15 yards from where he fiddled with the crossbow.

If Max snuck back around the front of the cabin and came in through the front door, he could find his 22 rifle, in the wardrobe and then quietly go to the medicine cabinet in the kitchen where he kept the bolt and ammunition. This way he would be armed enough to take on the situation and win.

He knew, however, that one of the codes of any commando was to ensure that all known weapons should be disabled in any raid that was to take place.

He believed that Felax would already have smashed the rifle and scattered the bullets to the 22. He didn't have time to test his theory as the huge man had suddenly jumped to his feet. Had he seen Max or felt the threat that hid less than 15 yards from him?

He charged down the backyard towards Daisy screaming obscenities in English and Yugoslav. "You fucking bitch you like that Max doodle no problems. Hump, hump then slide down for yum, yum and you don't think I see or hear?" His screaming had reached fervour pitch.

He stopped three feet in front of the inert Daisy and reached out with his empty hand. He gently lifted her face and lent forward and planted a kiss on her red lipstick covered lips. "See nice and easy," he had dropped his voice back to normal and appeared to be getting control of his rage.

Max hoped that shortly he could come out of hiding and talk the big man down.

"I show my love and softness towards you with a little kiss and what do you do in return?"

He looked around and patted his clothes then strode urgently back towards the house. He reached across the table and wrenched the hunting knife from its embedded position, wiped both sides on his trousers and ran back to where Daisy was still trapped against the tree.

As he approached, he lost all self-control and began to shout and gesture with the knife. "I offer you big hard cock one that would reach to the pleasure places of your body and give you orgasms and you slap my face you fucking bitch."

Max could see where this was heading as he had heard the stories from the Slav on many occasions.

He never thought to believe them always thinking that the actions were fabricated as he could never imagine any human being treating another as was described.

Sure enough the ex-soldier turned the hunting knife around so he grasped it by the blade.

Max recalled the stories while at the same time determining that he had to act and act fast.

Felax had often told how his band of renegades, acting on behalf of the Yugoslav Army but with full independence would seek out women and juice them up using the hilt of their hunting knives. Once this was accomplished, they would use the blade to act out the thrusting of a penis in love making. The poor woman would be sliced internally while the men would get themselves off on the power and the pain.

If they came upon a pregnant woman then she became part of a betting game with big money placed on the gender of the child. Of course, the only way to determine the winner was for the baby to be sliced from the womb.

The mother would die in agony as the winners gloated over their expertise and the money they had collected.

Felax once more lifted Daisy's head and placed the blade of the knife against her throat that's when Max knew the game was up. Even from the 50 yard distance the evidence was inescapable. The gold plating caught the sun and it flashed on and off.

The signet ring, held up by a piece of string, was hanging around her neck and. It shone brightly from the sun's rays catching it at the right angle.

"Damnation you cleaned up the evidence but forgot the most obvious. Fool, bloody simpleton." Max was now furious with himself.

The final plan was only in its embryo before Max acted. All he knew was that he had to stop Felax from touching Daisy with the hunting knife. As Max broke cover Felax began to lift Daisy's pretty floral dress.

Chapter 24

Max sprinted for the back verandah, intent on drawing Felax towards him. As he ran he fixed his eyes on the 303 rifle. He spun across the tabletop, grabbed the rifle and hit the floor heavily. In a bound he shot up and slammed the table onto its side and pushed the barrel of the rifle onto the upturned edge of the table. He peered through the V of the back sites searching to line up Felax, readying to squeeze off a round or two.

He quickly slid the bolt back to check that it was loaded and to his dismay found that there was only one bullet and that was already in the breech.

Nothing.

"Damn," he had under estimated the ex-commando and all the tricks the big bastard knew. "Where the hell did he get to?"

Max swept his eyes through the 180 degree view searching desperately. Then he caught a glimpse of the sharp needle like end of one of the bolts. It was pressed lightly into the left inside of Daisy's throat. A trickle of bright red contrasted with the ivory white of the woman's beautiful neck.

Felax yelled out gloatingly, "Got you Maxie boy. She's mine. With one shot of this bolt and you can do fuck all about it. Step out and walk this way you yellow little shit."

Max was thinking desperately as to what to do. There was still some doubt in the Slav's voice so maybe he believed there was a spare 303 bullet somewhere.

Next thing the right shoulder of Felax showed as a target to the left of the tree. This was a common trick to find out if your adversary had any weaponry that could do him any harm. The idea is to get the enemy to play their hand by shooting at the shoulder. There are no major organs in this area and the chances of hitting such a small target is low.

Even if a round was fired, it, still left Felax with a good left hand and a loaded crossbow. He was a mollydooker and from the range of 50 yards would not miss. One bullet fired and that would have left Max spent. He would be a dead man.

Max grabbed the chair nearby and spun to face the house. He charged at the window holding the chair like a battering ram. He hit the pane hard and the old, rotted putty cracked and fell away. The window pane crashed to the floor into a thousand pieces.

Max didn't miss a beat as he ran for the open front door and into the sunlight.

Ahead some 80 yards was the first of the trees that made up a remnant of the rainforest that once grew luxuriously throughout this area. He was trying to work the sums as to how long it would take Felax to cover the distance from the tree where Daisy was to the front of the house and let fly with the crossbow.

Max thought he might make the safety of the tree ahead with a second or two to spare.

As soon as Felax realised that Max was going to escape he tore around from behind the tree and set off at a lumbering pace to the right of the house. He was a huge man but once he was mobile, he covered the ground fast with gigantic steps. Ahead he glimpsed Max about to throw himself into the bush and fired the crossbow from the hip.

The bolt flew true and slammed into the tree inches from Max's head. A chunk of yellowish bark splintered off and whacked Max in the side of the head dazing him slightly. The bolt stuck two inches into the weeping wood of the trunk.

"Missed, but not next time you bastard," yelled a breathless Felax. He stopped to reload and Max made well his escape.

Logically it is quicker to move downhill using gravity to pull you along and this is what Max was hoping Felax would think.

Out of sight and in the tangle of undergrowth Max turned up hill, sprinting for his life. He reached the highest point and urged himself to climb a tall thick palm tree.

It was an old trick he had learnt from the indigenous people of the Daintree when they hunted for the beautiful orchids that hoisted themselves high in trees. The local birds helped by eating the seeds and then depositing them in the canopy.

At 30 feet he could see that Daisy was still tied to the tree. In the front yard he could see Felax bent over spent from running. Max had won so far now there was nothing left but to save his own hide and get out of this Hellhole. Daisy was a lost cause unless Felax had a change of mind.

He scrambled from the tree and set off to the north. Felax would have believed he was cutting down the slope and then turning south. That would eventually lead him into the caldera that had Mount Warning as its gigantic plug for the super volcano that had erupted a million or so years ago.

Max pushed on bearing North for two days then and only then did he feel safe enough to turn to the west. The daily rate of progress he had calculated to be fifteen miles so with two days of trudging through the MacPherson Ranges he estimated he was thirty miles west and thirty miles north of the cabin. He also had worked out he would pass to the west of Mount Warning if he turned to the south. By keeping away from people he would be safe enough to hop over the border and from their catch a lift into New South Wales. His disappointment was the loss of his motor bike.

Chapter 25

Daisy was lucky that Max had arrived back when he did. Without his appearance Felax was in such a stinking mood that he would have hurt her for sure. It was as if he was reliving the times in Yugoslavia when he was free to brutalise anyone.

She was particularly shocked when she looked into Felax's eyes as they were glazed and blood shot, as if the capillaries had burst due to the pressure he was exerting on his body.

Felax left Daisy roped to the tree for over an hour after he had run off after Max. From his later description it was apparent to Daisy that he had had a minor heart attack. He had flopped onto the grass after firing his bolt from his crossbow then felt a pain in his left arm.

After a long time he seemed to recover and get his temper under control. He came back to her all apologetic and sweet as he could be. He untied her and took her inside as you would expect of a gentleman.

Daisy wondered at times of his changed moods whether he was afflicted with schizophrenia.

Daisy heard no more from or about Max which was a pity as she had found him a delight to have around.

⧜

Detective Sergeant Doritich had copied down notes which were over and above what Daisy had put in her statement. He had found over the years that this was quite common.

He asked to speak to Felax and others who were at the township while Max J was living there. The men were all reluctant to become involved and spent their time giving mono-syllabic answers.

The detective located the Tiger 100 and took photographs for the Max Johnson file. He wasn't all that sure the information he had weaned out of the community matched his Max.

The timing and location were wrong. The motor-bike was correct although a proper identification could not be done as the licence plates were missing thanks to Felax and his mistrust of cops. He had unscrewed them and diced them in the lake near the cabin.

When the Missing Persons Bureau team went back to Brisbane Detective Sergeant telephoned Burton Johnson to keep him abreast of the case and to spread the news to others in the family.

Burton sat quietly listening to all the information and then let out an expletive followed by. "I suggest you get a few more police involved and find my son. During our last conversation you were telling me Max was in Townsville now he's in bushland south of Brisbane. Is he actually alive because that is what the family are saying?"

∞∽

Daisy had finished her story about Max J and turned to the second unlikely sighting which was in fact a second-hand information.

She told Doritich about her half yearly visits to the little settlement of Christmas Creek up in the MacPherson Ranges a few months after Max vanished. She had a girlfriend in the forest settlement. She heard what she believed could have been the next episode of the young Max's story.

Sandra Stephens had met a man wandering around and offered him a cuppa and a talk. The story she heard after she was told his name was Max had the same hallmark as the 'Numinbah Max'.

Sandra began her story telling to Ma Bertoli.

"As he travelled, through the forest of the MacPherson Ranges he came upon several wooden humpies that were scattered in the area. Most had been used by the timber cutters before being abandoned as the industry died out. Others had been taken up by squatters hiding from modern society for all sorts of reasons mostly unlawful.

"One of these shacks caught Max's eye as he ran past. He stopped and noted men's washing on the line and a vegetable garden out the back. He had a thought and went quickly to the door and knocked. He persisted for over a minute and called out, "Anyone about?"

"He opened the door and went inside. The interior was a shambles although in one corner was a neatly made bed. On the table were the leftovers of a hurried breakfast. Max rummaged around finding a loaf of damper, couple of tins of baked beans and a tin of spam. He grabbed an empty sugar bag and stuffed these items inside.

"As he went to go out the back door he spied a tin with the letters T-E-A on it. He snatched this from the shelf and put it in the sack.

"The vegetable garden was overgrown with weeds but several onions and some radishes were easily found and added to the bag of goodies. Max was finding a veritable treasure. He trotted to the clothes line and pulled off a pair of overalls and a ripped towel. The dolly pegs sprung loose and the items added to the sugar bag.

"Max knew he was now set for the challenge of fighting his way west through the rainforest and then turning south to come out near his grandmother's town of Tyalgum. He had all the provisions he needed and extra to boot.

"Max had been travelling for three days and was climbing higher into the mountains that surrounded Mount Tambourine. He was a survivor when it came to the rainforest so he had no doubts that by moving towards the south-west he would eventually cross the state border, find a lift and high tail it to Sydney.

"He was aware that the best place to get lost is where there are nearly a million people. An extra one means nothing and the others are all too busy living their own lives to be bothered with anyone else.

"As he moved stealthily along the ridge he looked out across the tree tops and could see some 500 yards away what looked like a scar on the landscape. Seemed to Max that a strong wind had smashed through the forest and snapped the vegetation off at an angle to the ground.

"He recalled the 1934 cyclone that he and his family had faced up in the Daintree and how one old red cedar had fallen and caused a swathe of forest to follow. This was different and he now started to believe it could have been a meteor.

"He should have stayed on the southerly course he had chosen but curiosity always gets to the best of us. He selected a land mark nearby, a huge tree that had fallen and been caught in the other trees. It was easy to spot because of the odd lean it had developed.

"He set off down the valley making for the odd smashed forest way on the far side of the valley. It was tough going as the slope was steep and underfoot was wet and slippery.

∞

"Max plodded on all day and reached the creek at the bottom of the valley just on nightfall. Here he moved across and about 50 yards up the other side. He needed to stay high enough above the creek because he knew how quickly flash floods could form further up the ranges and the devastating power they had. He bedded down for the night, hoping that tomorrow he would solve the intriguing mystery further up the mountain slope.

"He was up and on the move before the sun rose in the east. His time in the army taught him to be up early and use the coolness to cover distances. It was less exhausting and if the day became hotter dehydration would become a concern. The climb took a lot of energy but after six hours he found what he was searching for. He looked back across the valley and could make out the old leaning tree he had selected as a landmark. From where he stood, he calculated he was in the middle of the smashed forest. Above he could see the broken, splintered timber and further along the forest seemed to be devoid of trees. He searched round and was surprised to start finding pieces of metal. The further he walked the more things he found and then he came across an engine with a twisted propeller. He was so shocked that he gasped aloud, "My God, it's an aeroplane and the only one I know that crashed down here was a Stinson."

"He squatted on the ground and gazed around trying to remember the story of the crash and the heroic rescue that took place.

"An Airlines of Australia crashed into the mountainous area of the MacPherson Ranges on the 19th February, 1939. It was a Stinson Model A carrying two pilots and five passengers. One pilot and two passengers perished.

"The wreckage was later found by Bernard O'Reilly of the Lamington Guest House. This was an adventure worth the telling but the main drama was on the ground where four people desperately tried to stay alive and one made a dash to get help only to come to grief himself.

"The two pilots knew of some turbulence before taking off from Archerfield Airport at Brisbane but determined it to be minor. However, immediately retracting the wheels the aircraft ran into almost cyclonic weather. What went on in the cockpit was never determined. The aeroplane was reported missing at 7.30 pm on Friday and a full-scale search was instigated.

"The search area was centred in northern New South Wales but was proved to be inaccurate. Bernard O'Reilly made several visits around his locality to hear if anyone had heard an aeroplane circling in the MacPherson Ranges. From his information he believed the Stinson had come down further west than his Guest House. He set out to see if he could find the crew and passengers.

"The living two men were pleased to see him when he finally thrashed his way through the thick jungle. They told him a third victim had set off to walk out and get help. O'Reilly followed the man's trail only to find his body propped against a boulder.

"O'Reilly, with the help of a nearby Christmas Creek settlement managed to save the other two members on the Stinson's Passengers' List".

Max was presently sitting in the middle of the crash of that ill-fated aeroplane. The night was fast taking the sunlight so Max built a fire to stay warm. He couldn't explore or set off to the south until morning. He only hoped that Felax was not insane enough to have tried to track Max because he would arrive in a murderous mood.

The fire roared into life as Max fed more dry wood into the flames. The shadows produced by the dancing flames left eerie figures as though they were the passengers in ghostly form still trying to attract attention to their plight.

Max cuddled in to himself, moved close to the fire and in minutes fell into a deep sleep.

The Missing Persons' Unit had aready laid Max Johnson to rest and this story indicated nothing more than a stranger wandering the area in the MacPherson Ranges. To keep things simple Doritich only addded to the Max Johnson report "Homeless hiker seen in Christmas Creek".

Daisy stopped the story and added, "My next sighting was in the town of Uki. It is in the Mount Warning caldera volcano area. The story came from the lady who ran the boarding house on the out-skirts of the town. She showed me a photograph of a young chap on a Triumph Tiger 100 and the resemblance was uncanny. Her story was far more dramatic than I expected and the ending was sad. The police accepted her ending as proof that the MJ was Max Johnson and he was killed in an accident. This is the Uki story as best as I can recall what Ma Bartoli told me.

I wrote the story as I told it to the lass from Numinbah and I have a copy for the police," Ma Bartoli told Doritich.

⁓o⁓

This is the story that was placed in the file headed Johnson, M. Daisy wrote as she recalled.

The sleepy town of Uki was rudely awaken one frosty morning by the roaring of a motorcycle. The light sleepers heard the engine screaming from beyond the hill that dominated the landscape.

Uki was back behind the ranges but a long way south of where the Stinson had crashed.

Other residents awoke sleepy eyed wondering what was making the infernal racket. Peace to this town was one of their blessings and they were none too keen to have a troop of bikers in town although if they spent well, behaved and left by nightfall it would be a boost to the economy.

Ma Bertoli was already up and about cleaning the boarding house she kept just outside of the main town. Her abode was the first one that travellers passed as they came into Uki. It was on a sweeping bend and the Road Board had kindly made the road edges wider so that her boarders could park safely from the main traffic. Not that there was much traffic as the main road fizzled out barely two mile the other side of town, becoming a bush track fit for horses and dare devil motorbike riders. The track meandered into the mountains and became impassable.

Ma looked out the front window and watched the Triumph Tiger 100 cruise past, the rider sitting upright gunning the engine. He was putting on a show and doing it nice and slowly, letting all and sundry know that he had arrived. Ma made the sign of the Devil with her right hand and pretended to spit in the direction of the newcomer.

Further down the road was a petrol station come mechanic garage, a bakery, newsagent and further along a saw mill. A few wooden houses were scattered about the valley and some had smoke rising lazily into the cold, crisp air.

The biker did a sweeping U turn and pulled up at the bowser of the petrol station. Billy Joss sauntered out from the garage wiping his grease covered hands with a grey piece of flannelette.

"G'day mate ya want it filled up?" he asked.

The biker kicked the wheel stand down and dismounted. Steam billowed from the engine as the heat hit the cold air of the mountains.

"Ye mate, top her up. Nice little town you've got here. Have many visitors?"

Billy was a good mechanic but preferred to keep his conversations at a minimum. He found the stranger's questioning troublesome but answered with a grunt and followed this with, "Nah."

The rider noted Billy's reluctance to strike up a conversation and did not presss him. He was a typical country boy who preferred his own company. One that you would find in the pub with a schooner on the bar and as a solidary figure.

To pass the time the bikie took a 360 degree look at the panorama. The most eye-catching object was a mountain peak about twenty miles away. It was steep and forest covered. At the top was a rock column piercing the sky. Having read about Queensland's volcanoes he recognised it as Mount Warning. It was the plug left after a massive volcano had erupted millions of years ago.

By moving his eyes further to the west and north he could see the rim of what was left after the super volcano had taken all the rock, soil and vegetation and tossed it to the east. He stood in awe, nodding as he let his mind envisage the colossal volcanic eruption.

Mount Vesuvius, Krakatoa, Mount Etna and Mount Popocatepetl were written about because they were erupting in the modern era but few people knew about such super eruptions as Mount Warning.

The mechanic still remained silent so the biker asked, "Any place I can get a bed for the night or do I try the bush once again?"

This question was more to Billy's liking as he could see Ma Bertoli getting a few quid over and above her measly money from the two mill workers who boarded with her.

"Try Ma's back down the road. Only house on the right, ya came past it." Billy heard the petrol gurgling in the petrol tank and pushed a finger in to feel for the level. He drained a few more drops out before hanging up the hose and saying, "Two pound two and six, mate. Can I get you anything else? Something to eat or drink?"

The stranger took out a black leather wallet and stripped off three pounds from a wad of notes. Billy flicked his eyes to the wad and then the wallet and noticed an MJ embossed on the leather. He was about to make a guess at the name but then held his silence. He wasn't all that trusting of outsiders and this one made him more uneasy than most. The way he had signalled his arrival with the gunning of the motorbike engine, the wad of money, a bushy black beard covered by a red bandana and shifty eyes.

"Be seein' ya," said the stranger as he mounted the bike, pushed the wheel stand up and kick started the engine. He set off towards Ma's house ready for a good sleep as he had been on the road all night. The demons had not caught him and now he felt safe way out of their reach. This could be just the place to lay low for a few months.

Ma Bertoli had watched all the goings on down the road at the service station from her upstairs bedroom window. She was now watching the powerful motorbike making its way back towards her place.

She quietly hoped the scruffy, bearded rider, who reminded her of a picture of Ned Kelly the notorious bushranger down in Victoria, would ride on by and leave the town in peace. He looked like bad news and they didn't have any police or lawmen to deal with ruffians. On the other hand, she hoped he would pull the motorbike into her parking area and stay for a month or two as she desperately needed the money.

Ma smiled as the biker slowed and turned into her parking area. He turned off the engine, kicked the wheel stand down and dismounted. He stretched dramatically and pulled down the zipper on his black leather jacket which he removed and slung across his left arm. The next part of becoming a civvy was to remove the black helmet and place it on the pillion seat. He untied the red bandana and then looked up, feeling as though someone was watching him.

Ma shot backwards away from the window and grabbed up the broom. She bustled her way downstairs and opened the front door. The stranger was standing on the bottom step with his right arm outstretched and his fist balled about to knock.

"Heard you from miles away. You're making enough noise to waken the dead, may God rest their poor souls," said Ma. "I'm Ma," she said and shot out a hand in welcome.

The stranger took her hand in his, turned it slowly over and dipping his head forward gave it an exaggerated kiss. "Nice to make your acquaintance, my lovely woman. I am Mervin and I hear from the nice mechanic you may have a room I could bed down for the night."

Ma was taken back by the softness of Mervin's hands, the tingling sensation of the kiss and the impeccable manners she was hearing. "Yes, certainly," she stammered and then her business sense kicked in. "You would be most welcome to stay for a month or two or even longer if you like a quiet, friendly little town."

Mervin walked back to the motorbike and untied the binder twine that held a small swag on the pillon seat. He tucked this under his arm and followed Ma through the house. He noted four doors opening from the passage they were moving along. At the final door Ma took out a bunch of keys. She peeled one off the ring and handed it to Mervin.

"Bed and breakfast is my specialty. I do breakfast and other meals as long as you book a day ahead. If you need your washing and ironing done I can do that for you as well. Please make yourself at home and when you are rested come and talk to me about how long you want to stay and I'll work out the costs."

Mervin pushed the key into the hole and turned the lock. As he entered the small, but comfortable room he turned back to thank Ma but she had gone. He threw the swag on the floor and sat tiredly on the bed. He pulled the heavy leather boots off and sunk his tired body into the kapok mattress. Within seconds he was snoring soundly.

∞∞∞

Mervin stayed in town for over six months and became quite a character. He did odd jobs around the saw mill and out in the forest where the felling took place. He helped at the local garage when Billy went on a bender or was unwell. All in all he became accepted although the townspeople, could not get used to the way he would roar the bike up and down the main street when he was in a mood or had too many schooners.

The local lasses found him to be worth their attention and loved to be given a ride on the pillion seat. Mervin was always the gentleman towards the girls, never trying anything that would make them fear him or be ashamed.

The latter behaviour started the town talking about Mervin's sexual preferences and one thing led to another and the community came up with the word homosexual. The problem with their thinking was that Mervin did not display any like or love for his fellow man. Some of the young girls decided that it was time to test the waters so they began to visit Marvin at the boarding house.

Ma wasn't too pleased with this turn of events but kept her silence as she had learnt early in her time in Uki that if you upset one person in town you upset them all.

Mervin was happy to have the girls visit and most did not push past his comfort zone. He was always courteous and conversational. He was a complete mystery and of course when a mystery is thrown into the mix everyone wants to be the one to solve it or be part of the whispered rumours.

One of Mervin's challenges around town was the mile straightaway that led out to the forest to the west. This was part of the road that led to a track and pushed high into the mountains and became impassable.

A few hundred yards the other side of town there was a mile long straight that ended at a bridge. The bridge had been made across a creek at a point where there was a short but steep ravine. From one side to the other was barely ten yards but the water that flowed swiftly was thirty feet below. The local pioneers of the town had dragged in by horse half a dozen huge cedar logs and using the granite rock on either side had fashioned a bridge. Across the logs they had nailed on flat six by two planks. It was a sturdy structure even though the planks created a burring sound as a motor was driven over them.

To make it attracting to the towns folk who would walk out that way for a picnic at a small pool above the ravine the timber workers had offered their time and timber to fashion a footbridge on one side. They built a walk way and two hand rails.

Mervin would be happy to take one of the girls for a spin or go solo out to the start of the "Mad Mile" as it became known. Here he would gun the Triumph Tiger 100 and flash through the trees until he rumbled across the bridge. The bridge being the end of the official race.

As he charged along he would count slowly and at the end would be elated if his final number was less than the best he'd done before. He would happily share his times and conquests with the pillion passengers. His record stood at 35 seconds that was assuming he counted at exactly one second at a time. To Mervin it mattered only that his numbers dropped and he was keen to get that to below 30.

Mervin told Ma one evening that when he was ready to move on his one farewell present was to do the mad mile under 30 seconds. He said that he'd have enough adrenalin to get him geed up and the wind rushing past his face would offer the little extra to tip the bike under 30 as he hit the finish line at the bridge.

∾o∾

One Sunday, nearly six months into his stay in Uki, the community had a party. It began with a few drinks at the local watering hole with extra members adding to the crowd. A keg was bought and the party spilt out onto the main street with tables and chairs for comfort. Some of the ladies rushed off home to cook up foods and these added to the merriment that was building. By nightfall most were tipsy and some quite drunk.

One of the girls was making a play for Mervin and was becoming more and more confident with her advances. She was the long haired blond called Cass, who knocked around Billy Joss's garage at odd hours. She didn't seem to do much in the way of mechanics or serving petrol. She spent most of her time ogling the passing timber workers and touching Mervin on the backside as she 'accidentally' brushed past.

Mervin was always pleasant and polite and didn't give her any reason to believe he enjoyed her advances. Billy, on the other hand, tried desperately to reach out to her and complimented her dress sense and beauty at every opportunity. She would giggle, turn up her nose and walk away wiggling her cute little bum. Billy's efforts had intensified in the past fortnight and at times Mervin felt there was an attraction growing but they didn't seemed to him to be at all suited.

Cass finally managed to drag Mervin away from the party and into the night. She began to passionately kiss him inserting her tongue deeply into his mouth.

Mervin had, in the whole time he had stayed, resisted the girls of the town and had kept his feelings under control. However, Cass's kissing was so frenetic, delightful, hot and full on that he found himself with a hard-on and was delighting in the attention.

"Take me back to your place," the girl said hoarsely and began to haul Mervin further into the night and away from the partygoers.

The two bodies crashed onto the bed in a flurry of arms, legs and clothing. The girl gave her body to Mervin who lost all sense of control and began to force himself inside of her. In his eagerness and the fact that he had not had sex for many months he ejaculated prematurely. Guilt rushed through his whole being and he rolled away.

The girl was disappointed but far from finished. She tried gallantly to arouse Mervin but to no avail. She pushed him onto his back and slid down passed his waist. She took his loose member in her tiny white hand and placed it into her mouth. She felt an arousal and thought she was on the road to victory.

Suddenly there was a loud ear-splitting shout and then the splintering of wood as the door exploded open and in charged Billy Joss. He was in a purple rage. "You dirty, fucking little bitch," he screamed and grabbed the girl by the long blond hair and tossed her at the wall. There was a sickening crunch as her petite, bare body slammed into the woodwork.

Mervin was transfixed trying to work out what the hell went wrong. One second, he was in paradise with hot, wet lips sucking his limp member and the next being bitten in the same place by the same body as she reacted to the violence that had been wreaked upon her.

Mervin jerked himself up and scrambled away but he was too late. Billy grabbed him by the beard and yanked him to his full height of five foot ten. He punched him flush on the nose, cartliage snapping and blood spurting all over the bed and Mervin's naked body.

"She was mine, you bastard, she was mine. We were going to be married next month. Now you fucked her I don't want the bitch. As for you if you are still in town by sun up I'll come after you with the double barrel shot gun."

Billy turned his attention to the girl who lay unconscious against the wall. He picked her up gently and stepped back. He pulled the sheet from the bed and wrapped it around her naked body and walked to the door all the time blubbering and whispering, "I loved you. I loved you. I wanted you. How could you do this to me?"

Then they were both gone.

Mervin cleaned himself up and put on new clothes. He was still very groggy from the booze and the belting. He knew he had blown any chance of staying in Uki so it was time to move on.

He took out his wallet and peeled off £20 that he placed on the sideboard. He scribbled a note for Ma to say sorry about the situation, the mess and the fact that he had to leave. As he made for the door, he had a change of mind and went back to the sideboard. He took out the wallet and replaced the £20 with a five and carefully placed the wallet on the wooden top so that the embossed letters MJ were clearly visible.

He rolled up his swag and went out to the bike. He placed himself astride of the Triumph Tiger 100 when it occurred to him that by now the townsfolk would know the story and be coming out on Billy's side. If they heard the bike, they might pursue him and that could be dangerous.

He got off, kicked the wheel stand up and pushed the bike back along the road out of town. It was hard, heavy work but he persisted. He had gone over a hundred yards and was now on a slight rise. He looked back and could see that the party had broken up and there were few people milling around.

A new idea began to form in his fuzzy head. He would push the bike off the road and have a rest until he was sure everyone was in bed. When he was sure it was all quiet and he was free to move he would put his plan in place.

⟆⟆

Mervin must have dozed for a period because when he looked up he could make out the sun's rays peeking over the eastern ranges.

He sprung to his feet and was surprised that he felt so much better than last night after Billy had snotted him. He gingerly felt the tip of the nose and it was tender. He stood the motorbike up and turned it around, facing back to town. He pushed it forward, ran a few steps then jumped on to the seat. The gravity and the slight slope allowed the bike to coast along back through town. It picked up a little speed as it coasted silently through the lightening darkness.

As the momentum slowed Mervin jumped off and kept pushing. With determined effort he got the bike to the start of the "Mad Mile". Now he would prove to all and sundry, including himself, that he was the Under 30 champion of the World.

He jumped on the bike, kicked it into life and revved the throttle. He loved the sound and so he gunned it a second time before flicking it into gear. The bike shot off and Mervin started counting. At the same time, he flicked the bike through the gears and watched the speedometer climb dramatically.

✺

Back in town most people were fast asleep, oblivious to the drama taking place just outside the town limits. The three people who thought they heard the roaring of a motorbike weren't prepared to say with certain as it sounded some way off.

Mervin was in his element as the cold wind slammed into his exposed beard. He loved the speed and the sound of the Triumph Tiger 100 when it was at its peak.

22, 23, 24……ahead he could just make out the bridge and he felt a tingling run up his spine as he estimated he was ahead of the 30 mark.

25, 26, 27…..He was almost there and victory was his. He could hear the crowds shouting his name and whistling his praise.

28, 29….the bike slammed into the wooden palings of the footbridge. They splintered and a huge chunk impaled Mervin's left leg tearing his femoral artery and smashing the femur in several parts. The front wheel of the bike caved in as the spokes sprung out from the impact. The back of the bike overtook the slowing front and the bike turned a full somersault into the void that was the ravine. The swirling waters and rocks below became a watery grave for Mervin and his beloved Triumph Tiger 100.

∾o∾

Mervin had left town and the people signed a relief.

Ma said her one puzzle was to get an answer to whether he carried out his last wish before leaving Uki. He told her he wanted to go with an under 30 second ride over the mad mile. After he disappeared, she had wandered to the bridge and saw the smashed railing and wondered if it was Mervin's very last wish or did someone else remove that piece of the wooden bridge?

Ma mentioned in her story that the ravine had swelled with the rain of the winter and the water level had remained near the bottom of the bridge for most of Spring.

With the onset of a dry Spring coupled with a nil rainfall in Summer the creek dried and the waterfall ceased gushing down the ravine. The locals were excited to see what the river system looked like so they scrambled to the bottom and fossicked around. It was not going to be too long before one and two would chance upon Max's skull and more of the Triumph Tiger 100.

∾o∾

It was a Friday afternoon and knock off time was fast approaching much to Detective Sergeant Tom Doritich's delight when he was interrupted by a member of his team.

"What's on your mind Filmer?"

"Sorry to bother you, boss but the locals of Uki have just turned up a skull. Add to that a motorcycle and a few scattered human bones and we may have a murder victim or at the least a missing person."

"Damn, I thought we did a thorough job of that body and motorbike. So is this going to prove Max Johnson is still alive or was he killed in that accident? Let's get the team together," said Doritich and jumped up, grabbed his deep blue suit coat and followed his junior officer from the building.

The two men picked up a black FX holden from the car pool and drove around to the forensic section of the Police Department which was located in the Brisbane Hospital.

Doritich sort out two of the staff, Roger Jones a skilled forensic investigator and Peta Savoury a micro-biologist. These two would check around the site and collect samples from the body and the motorbike.

In the meantime, Doritich and Constable Matthew Filmer drove back from the site and into

Uki. They would spend a few days interrogating the locals to see if they could get a match with other people who had been involved with the police over the past.

Chapter 26

The evidence of a fatal crash at the bridge was found by a group of locals going on a picnic. As summer burst upon the town and the surrounding mountains the amount of precipitation diminished and the creek fell to its lowest level ever.

The group of townspeople was walking across the bridge seeking to find a picnic spot further on. A young lad began throwing stones into the ravine. One stone made a metallic sound and so on investigation the boy was shocked to spy the wheel of a motorbike.

Billy Joss was summoned and asked to bring his tow truck which had an A frame and pulley attached, Billy parked the truck sideways in the middle of the bridge and ascended on the chain into the ravine. The onlookers were shocked when he called up, "My God it's a Triumph Tiger 100 and there are bones wedged in the rocks. Someone had better call the coppers."

Speculation was rife throughout the district as to who the skull belonged to and how the bicycle got to be smashed at the bottom of the ravine.

∽o∽

Detective Sergeant Tom Doritich from the Missing Persons Bureau in Brisbane who had been assigned the case of Max Johnson heard of the find and went out to Uki to investigate. Ma swears that it was she who had alerted the officials. She was sure the body belonged to Mervin.

In the meantime, Doritich and Constable Matthew Filmer drove back from the site and into Uki. They would spend a few days interrogating the locals to see if they could get a match with other people who had been involved with the police over the past.

∞∞

Detective Doritich and his team arrived in Uki just before lunch time. They were hoping to get the investigation completed by night fall.

This short timeline became impossible when they arrived at the accident site. The mountain slope was steep and difficult to climb, the ravine the pieces of the motor bike and bones were found in was deep and the rushing of the water made it impossible to fossick for other evidence.

By mid afternoon the team met on the bridge to report what they had found and the progress they had made. Each agreed that they would need several days to thoroughly search all the evidence and come to a reasonable decision. Detective Doritich agreed and added that the assistance of the townspeople would be of use. He hired Billy and the tow truck to allow team members to reach into the depth of the ravine and to haul up parts of a Triumph Tiger 100 motorcycle.

After three extra days and staying with Ma Bertoli in her boarding house, the team retired to Brisbane. Their physical work at the Uki site was complete. Now they had to write up a full report and a conclusion. The typewriters in the office got a thorough workout and the two-hundred-page report ended with, "The evidence points clearly to the deceased being one Max Johnson who appears to have come to grief on the Uki Bush Bridge whilst riding his Triumph Tiger 100 at high speed. His parents will be notified and the case closed."

Burton Johnson was notified that the body parts and those of a Triumph Tiger 100 had been positively identified as those of Max Johnson. Marion had a break down and others were inclined to say, "I told you so", some blamed Burton, some Annette's mother.

A funeral was arranged and the forensic team organised for all of the pieces to be transferred to the white chapel to be interned. Max Johnson was found but gone.

∽∘∾

At a meeting between the four investigators, it was determined that they were dealing with a male, five foot ten inches, dark hair. rode a Triumph Tiger 100 motorcycle with little care for his own safety or others.

He was killed in an accident at least a year ago. If the initial crash didn't cause death, then he surely would have drowned within minutes of hitting the water in the pool below the bridge.

From the townspeople the only man who would fit the description was a bloke who had breezed into town last year. He was riding a Triumph Tiger 100 and had stayed at Ma's Boarding House then suddenly disappeared after an altercation over a young woman with one of the locals.

This person had left his wallet behind in his Boarding room. Neatly pressed into the leather of the wallet on the outside were two initials. The J was quite clear but not so the other which could have been N, M or even W.

Detective Sergeant Tom Doritich summed up what the team had discovered and then said, "The obvious person that ticks all the boxes is a young fellow who disappeared from his father's dairy farm in Kenmore two years ago.

He was called Max Johnson, hence the MJ on the wallet. Doritich summed up his second visit saying, "If we could have found the whole number plate of the motorcycle our evidence would have been complete.

I'll send our findings to the young constable at the Kenmore Police Station and he can visit the Johnson's and give them the sad news."

When the news hit the Johnson family, they took it really hard. Marion knew why Max has disappeared and was the only one who knew the whole truth. The argument between Max and Annette was the straw that broke the camel's back or she would have said the final point that pushed Max over the cliff. To Marion there was still one question she needed answering and that was, "Why did it take Max several months before he crashed the motor bike from the time he left the farm?"

She felt really sad that Max had left behind a daughter and a wife both who had little support. He didn't even leave anything behind for them and that was disappointing.

Burton shrugged his shoulders and walked away. He knew why Max had cleared off and his part in the young fellow's life was more his fault than anyone elses.

If he had listened to the boy's story about the crocodile in the billabong and questioned Keith closely he would have found the real culprit. Instead, he heard out the less trustworthy and set himself on a collision course with his youngest son.

∽o∾

All the girls wept buckets of tears. As much as Max could at times be bossy, he was good fun and loved to join into all the games they played. They would miss him terribly.

Burt, the oldest of the clan had already lost his best mechanic and now he knew that it could be permanent. He had to make do with the team he had built.

Max was gone so he had to pick up the pieces within the family and to at least make sure his new little niece was looked after. He went around to see Annette and tell her his plan but she got emotional and became argumentative. She finally told him to get out and never bother her again.

As Burt walked sullenly away from the flat Annette threw one last comment, "Keep your family well away from me and just for your information that gutless wonder you call Max was not my baby's father!" Burt swung back to continue the argument but Annette was gone.

That evening Burt went home to his wife Connie and told her what had transpired between himself and Annette.

Connie told him he must bite his tongue as the comment may have been made in revenge and was a lie or Annette wanted to stir up the Johnson family causing infighting. By keeping mum the whole emotional question would not need to be visited again.

Max's skull and some more pieces of his precious motor bike were buried behind the little white church on top of the hill at Kenmore. Marion was pleased that the final pieces of the puzzle were now with the rest and that this tranquil place would be his last.

Max could sit on the grave and look down into the valley and see everyone going about their businesses and make sure that no one was getting up to mischief.

Burt could not get it out of his head that Max would commit suicide and even worse that he would damage his pride and joy. The Triumph Tiger 100 was as precious to him as was the tennis ball he owned when they were kids in the Daintree.

Burt was determined to keep a lookout for his brother. He assembled his team and told them to ask questions about Max as they travelled the east coast in their semi-trailers.

Any information was going to help. The men agreed to the request but some whispered that Burt will need to accept that his brother was dead someday.

At every truck stop, motel and hotel the same questions were asked and Max's description was circulated. The year rolled by but nothing was forthcoming.

Was MJ dead or lost in the Queensland wilderness or had he started a new life and didn't want to be found?

❦

By the time Burt started to look seriously for his baby brother, Maxie Jebert had reached Toowoomba on his slow journey to Sydney. Was Maxie Jebert the man Burt and the police were seeking?

Burt did learn later that Maxie Jebert had a dark complexion, dark wavy hair and rode on a Tiger 100 motor bike. The part that didn't fit was a black moustache and the one thing Max detested was hair above the lip.

Toowoomba began a new chapter in Maxie Jebert's life one that was exciting but one that ended up disastrous. It was a large town and the commercial side contained every industry that was required for a sheep and wheat farming area to exist happily.

He decided to hide amongst the big town population for a while. He went off around the farms to see what jobs might be available. After a dozen or so of negative answers he rode back to town to find a pub to book a room.

He had hardly cleaned his teeth when there was a loud and incessant knocking on the door. His first thought was police because the knocking was authoritarian like. He opened the door and a man in a long grey coat and a broad brimmed black hat stood there.

"You the bloke looking for a job?"

"Yes sir, Maxie Jebert," and he thrust his hand out. The response he got was a strong grip and a vigorous shaking.

"Nice to meet you Maxie. Name's Dion Gilbert. The job is on the wheat bins starting in the morning 7.30 am. The learning is on the job so turn up with a hat and boots ." With those terse words Dion Gilbert turned and left.

He knew Toowoomba was on the Darling Downs and this was a plain of rich soil. The agriculture industries were most important. Wheat and sheep abound along with flowers in the main town.

Max rode sedately into town and parked in the main street. A few onlookers were taken by the Triumph Tiger 100 but they observed from a distance. His biggest worry about these towns was that they were getting closer to Brisbane and the police force tended to be in the double figures.

As most were peaceful places any unusual happening could be quickly investigated by several coppers. He had to be careful not to bring attention to himself nor get into a conversation with people who may start asking questions. So far, the outback people had tended to keep to themselves and left strangers and passersby to themselves.

He found a café and ordered a strong black coffee and two slices of carrot cake His memories were waning as the years ebbed by and even the taste of scones with strawberry jam and cream did not make him react as might be expected.

Max had planned a medium length stay before moving on to the east. He booked into the local caravan park and paid for a caravan to cover three weeks. He parked the Triumph Tiger 100 on the door side in easy reach if anyone dared to try to ride off on it.

After several hours resting Max felt hungry so decided stroll around the town to see what other delights he could find. A nice hot dog or meat pie and tomato sauce would be ample.

He walked along the main street taking in the sights and sounds. The horses to machines change was almost done.

An elderly couple dressed in black came clip clopping in a horse drawn buggy down the street just to emphasize that some of the elderly folk could not move that last step. These people were Mormons from a peaceful religious Sect. Two young fellows talking a little louder than necessary made mention of those left in the horse age. They had refused to take up the motor driven machines and so used the horse as a mode of transport and farm work.

After a brief look around he noticed a sign in a shop window that mentioned Ravensbourne Park and there being two magnificent redwood trees growing in it. He made haste to his motorbike and set off to a place called Ravensbourne National Park.

He hadn't seen these towering beauties since leaving the Daintree in 1936. He was looking forward to a bit of nostalgia. He saw the trees before he realised he had reached the park. They stood straight and tall, towering over all the other vegetation in their surrounds. It would seem that this clump of redwoods had been left by the lumberjacks half a century ago because they weren't worth getting out. Now they were magnificent.

Maxie dismounted from the Triumph Tiger 100, sat it on the stand and went to each tree and gave them a hug. He could barely get his outstretched arms a quarter of the way around. He looked straight up for over 30 yards and there was barely a branch all the way to the top. Maxie could see why these trees were so sort after by the English navy as masts for their sailing vessels.

After his visit to the redwood trees he rode back to the centre of town. He was pleased to notice a smell waft passed and he stopped to take a few more whiffs. The unmistakable aroma of bread, freshly made ascended into his nose.

Chapter 27

After a few weeks working on the Wheat Bins Maxie moved south to the town of Dubbo. Here fate dealt a hand in his love life. He had promised himself to stay clear of the female sex as they had proved too dangerous for him.

Maxie pulled up in the centre of Dubbo, dismounted and set off in search of a shop that sold coffee and cakes. He soon spied the place he hoped would be selling sweet cakes. It was a Bakery but also baked sweet cakes and sold coffee, tea, milk shakes and cool drinks.

He moved towards the door and was confronted by a young lady in a hurry. She had materialised from the shop next door and was carrying a silver tray above her head. Maxie tried desperately to avoid a collision but the girl did not, pressing onwards. The silver tray shot out of her hand and a large pig's head flew towards the Bakery.

Maxie was full of apologies and offered his hand to the girl so that he could help her from the footpath. As she came to a standing position Maxie realised she was wearing the uniform of a butcher. Her apron was striped blue and white and she wore high rubber boots. A scarf held her hair in place and away from dangers such as circular saws, mincers and sausage making machines.

Maxie bent and picked up the silver tray then set off after the pig's head which he retrieved and replaced on the tray.

"My apologies madam," said Maxie. "How can I make up for my clumsiness."

Much to Maxie's surprise the girl answered confidently, "I'm Danielle the butcher's daughter and you may carry the tray inside for me and give the head a good washing with hot water. Once finished I will continue my errand and then you can take me for lunch at the Royal Café further along the street and tell me your life's story."

With all of that and Maxie in a clear understanding of the girl's wishes she marched back to the butcher's shop and held the door open.

As he moved past she asked, "Do you perchance have a name or can I make up my own?"

"Max," he said then added, "Maxie , Max Jaxon." The question on everyone's lips in Dubbo would become, "Was this his real name or an alias?"

∽o∾

This was the start of a relationship that at times had the makings of a romance and at other times a brawl in a boxing ring scheduled for three rounds.

Danielle and Maxie started as two distant lovers then every now and again she would fly off the handle at the silliest things and Maxie would give her a cold shoulder for days on end.

Her love in life was going wild pig hunting with 'the boys'. She was a driver of a utility all decked out for pig shooting. While she was tearing across paddocks with a dozen pigs squealing in the spotlight, she was one of the boys and over the moon happy.

When she was at home seeking Maxie to stay over night and he offering an excuse for going home she would lose her temper and call him names his mother would never allow in her home.

Next day she would be all over Maxie and loving him as though nothing had happened. Maxie spent his days wondering whether this day was on or off and at times rueing the day he met this firebrand.

The relationship would take a special young female to pry it open. One who was the total opposite to the personality of Danielle.

Only one person in Dubbo knew the real name of the man who rode a Triumph Tiger 100 and loved the young girl from the Dubbo Butcher's Shop.

Was this one the real Max Johnson or another with the initials MJ as he signed when he turned up for the job on the Petrol Station at Dubbo. They had met in unusual circumstances so maybe it was fate working with him. The forward part of his story began when he left Dubbo. He was going to start a new life in Sydney with his girl Danielle. She had barged into his life and she had that dare devil sense of living just like Max had.

Max Johnson's complicated life and story was far from complete even though the Missing Persons' Bureau had closed his case and stamped the report DECEASED.

Another part of his story was being played out in another town in another state of Australia. The main characters did not know Max Johnson and it would be a little while before parts of the Max Johnson jigsaw would start to click together.

Werrimull is a tiny location on the map of Victoria close to the Murray River. The Murray was a magnificent River and its watershed was in the Australian Alps. The many streams that fed the Murray came from the snow country and then the wheat and sheep country as it flowed across Victoria and South Australia. Its potential as an irrigation farmland was seen by two Chaffey brothers, George and William, who came up the river to Mildura in 1887. They were Canadian migrants searching for the ideal to set up farming that would see the area become the fruit and vegetable basket of Australia. The amount of water that flowed through Mildura was enormous.

It wasn't long before small plots were being cleared and ploughed. Grapes, citrus fruit and vegetables were planted and watered by irrigation. At first pipes were used but as more and more land was planted the need for water increased so irrigation channels were dug. These criss-crossed the landscape for miles around the growing town of Mildura.

Once the plants reached maturity the fruit and vegetables were picked and sent down stream to Echuca and transported into the growing city of Melbourne. The fruits and vegetables were delicious and juicy. The irrigation system was successful and expansion would keep up with the population growths of Melbourne and the other Australian cities.

Werrimull was too far from the river so its water was from dams and bores. It was cattle country supplemented by grain, mainly wheat and oats.

German people who worshipped in the Lutheran Church around about 1845 were leading a devoted spiritual life based on the Lutheran Doctrine. There was a small group that objected to the difference of the interpretation over how that faith was to be formally expressed in worship services. The unhappiness that resulted caused a schism. Some of the Lutheran Church members immigrated to South Australia to a new life.

The settlers who were being persecuted by the conservative Lutherans begun wholesale migration to Adelaide the capital of South Australia. Some remained on the Adelaide Plains to grow grapes and make wine. Others ventured east and north into the Wimmera to fatten cattle for beef.

In amongst the farms that were being cleared and readied for cropping there lived a family called Henschke. There were 5 girls and 7 boys and they grew into adulthood determined to marry and continue the farming plans that their forebearers had laid out. One of the Henschke children was a young lady called Edna.

Edna was full of energy and fun. She was mother's helper as she grew into a teenager. Then she met and married Thomas Adams from Meringur and he insisted the newly married couple move to Merbein near Mildura. The cottage was ample for two but Edna soon discovered she was pregnant with a boy. The family grew from one to four with Jimmy, Ken, Ron and Joy coming in quick succession.

Unfortunately, the marriage did not flow as gently as the Murray River.

Thomas had a roving eye and his head was especially turned by the young girls of the towns of

Mildura and Merbein. He would meet with each of the Henschke girls at pre-determined times and any day during the week. The girls were just as keen to learn what life was all about. They would saddle a horse out on the farm and with an excuse to visiting a friend in town would ride the 20 miles in to meet up with Thomas.

Edna was aware of the shenanigans of her wayward husband but too frightened to confront him. He had a fiery temper and was willing to use physical force to get his way or silence an adversary.

The couples only daughter, Edna Joyce (shortened to Joy) grew up with three boisterous brothers and lots of friends who all attended the Merbein School. She was so loved by her mother and protected from any boy with evil intent.

Thomas, as the father, was happy to whisper goodnights and chat with his daughter. The relationship became more worrying as Joy grew into a teenager. With the freedom that he used to meet up with the Hensckhe girls Thomas desired the same with his daughter. Edna would have none of that and kept a fierce eye on any physical contact between father and daughter.

For her vigilance and willingness to stand up to the physically stronger Thomas, Edna copped many beatings. One of Thomas's favourite method of dealing with Edna was to wait for lunch time when his wife would go to the house to make lunch.

Earlier before leaving for the vineyards Thomas would have let out his plan for the day. This usually included not being home for lunch. He would then arrive and surprise Edna, grab her hair and force her onto the kitchen floor and have his way with her. It was brutal and uncalled for but he wanted her to know that she was under his power at all times.

Edna had matured over the 13 years of her marriage and was prepared to stand up to her demanding husband. She accepted the violence that was at times unleashed but never wavered from her stance. All the while she worked long hours in the vineyards.

Joy was blossoming into a beautiful young lady with a delightful laugh. She was very quiet and timid and obedient to her mother. Her father was beginning to show an interest in her which bothered Edna.

Edna was working in the next-door neighbour's vineyard one day when a tall rangy gentleman came sauntering to where she was trimming the old vines back. He politely introduced himself and started a conversation. Edna was taken by the calm temperament of her visitor. He finally decided to move on so he said goodbye and left.

∞∞

The next day the visitor introduced himself. "Hello there I'm Matthew Koch. I'm working on a block further to the east. It belongs to the blockee, Albert Gebur."

Edna was pleased to see Matthew and introduced herself to him, "I'm Edna Adams."

Matthew began to make it a habit to arrive where Edna was working and chat away to her. His temperament was so pleasant after what she was used to from her husband that she was always happy to see him.

∞∞

As the days turned to weeks Edna and Matthew became friends who could talk about anything. They never judged each other nor disagreed with the other's stance on topics. The discussions became deep and secrets were swapped.

One day at lunch time, Edna had found Thomas waiting in the kitchen and she knew what his intention was so she braced herself and he attacked. During the pushing, slapping and punching Thomas blackened Edna's eye. The next day Matthew was horrified to see Edna's face and in particular her eye. He managed to get the full story from her including the history of her marriage.

Matthew began to pursue the idea of her leaving her marriage but she couldn't because she had taken the marriage vow – "Until death do us part."

At about the same time as Edna was telling Matthew about her marriage the growing family looked for ways to be more social. The belief that Edna was coming up with was if she and the children were with other people then her wayward husband wouldn't hurt any of them. His goody reputation would need to be kept intact.

The idea worked as expected but the bashings continued just at a different time. Like all bullies Thomas had an appetite to use his power and fists to pick victims who did not fight back.

One of the ideas was to join an indoor carpet bowling club. They formed the backbone to a team called the Grapes of Wrathe.

The competition had just been set-up so there were some stragglers who needed to be placed in a team.

On the first night the Grapes of Wrathe showed skills that they were surprised they had. They won the rounds and were congratulated by all the other teams. The following week Edna caught sight of her visitor to the vineyard and approached him.

"Hello what are you doing here?"

"My brother and I would like to join a team and play competitively if we could only get an invitation."

Edna was keen to add a player or two to the Grapes of Wrathe. Matthew asked Edna to introduce him as Matty as that was his local nickname. She agreed and introduced Matty and Roy to the others and asked if they would mind adding the two to the team. This was readily accepted.

∽o∾

Matty soon became a confidante to Edna so much so she used him as a sounding board. She would work away at the job she was allocated and chat about all sorts of subjects. Slowly she began to get Matty's opinion as well as any solutions that might help.

Matty was sitting on his haunches in amongst the grapevines when he raised the question of the dinner time domestic violence that Edna was copping.

Edna turned to him and said, "I can put up with that it is my daughter that I am terrified for. Thomas has this determination to take every virgin he can find and abuse them on their sixteenth birthday. He has managed to do exactly that to every one of my sisters. I don't want it happening to my daughter."

Matty sat and said nothing but an embryo of a plan began to grow. As he left to go back to his job he stopped and turned to Edna with a question, "When does Joy turn sixteen?"

Edna replied, "18th November this year."

It was a night when the air gets to feel so thick with humidity and flashes of lightning lights the surrounds when Edna heard Joy scream. She dropped the mop which fell across her path. As she rushed forward, she tripped on the mop handle and crashed to the floor. Her outstretched arms pushed a chair over which in turn up-ended the bucket full of water.

The girl's plaintiff cry continued while Edna got to her feet and limped towards Joy's bedroom. As she reached the door, she was surprised to find it was closed. It was slung open and Thomas moved swiftly passed without a comment. Edna rushed in to find Joy sitting at the top of her bed on a pillow and holding both legs with her arms.

"Whatever is the matter, my dear?" implored Edna. Joy was still screaming but cut the scream short at the sound of her mother's voice.

"Dad was hurting me and wouldn't stop so I screamed to make him go away."

"What was he doing to you?"

The description of the visit by Thomas into Joy's room shocked Edna and she was furious. Not wanting the teenager to understand what her father was doing Edna hushed the girl, tucked her in and told her to go to sleep."

Edna rushed out in search of her husband. She was not only going to give him a piece of her mind but would threaten to report the incident, as described by Joy, to the police.

As expected, Thomas was nowhere to be seen and he did not return to the house that night.

The next day Edna sent Joy on her way to school and went off to continue her current job in the vineyard. Matty was already working on a block two further away than the one Edna was toiling on. Edna rushed to him sobbing out the story of what Thomas was doing in Joy's bedroom.

Matty calmed Edna and said, "You need to get the girl away from him before he does untold damage to her and ends up on the wrong side of the law. I'll help you if you see the truth in what I am telling you."

Edna looked up into his brown eyes and said, "Anything Matty, anything. You just say the word and I'll follow you to the end of the World to protect my daughter. I'm scared, really scared. You don't know Thomas but he has friends in every level of society in this town and he can readily obtain guns to shoot me. That's a threat he has used on occasions."

The couple went back to the work that had been allocated to them but all the while began to plan an escape from Merbein. The escape plan was worked on at lunch time.

Chapter 28

The final plan would need three weeks to be fully implemented. In the meantime, Edna had to keep an eye on Joy. At the end of the week the two girls would move into Edna's sister's house secretly and without fuss. They would stay for a week and then be spirited out of the district.

Matty was to scrape up whatever money he could from his savings and any of his friends who would take an IOU. He was not to tell anyone what was afoot.

He had a mate, Jim Jackson, who owned a caravan that he often told Matty he was welcome to borrow. There was some work that had to be done to make it roadworthy and safe. This would take at least a fortnight to fix. Once the caravan was ready it would be hooked to Matty's Holden and towed over to Robinvale and booked in the caravan park under Matty's name. It was to be there for a week and carefully watched to see if Thomas Adams or a friend of his would work out what it would be involved in. If there was no movements Matty would hitch it up and pick up the girls and head east.

The plan went smoothly although Thomas was furious when he discovered that Edna and Joy had vanished. His sons told him they watched their mother packing belongings. They said she offered them a choice of going on a trip to Melbourne or staying in Merbein with their father before she was taken away by one of Edna's brothers. They didn't know her destination.

After the first week of the plan Thomas began to feel pleased with his new freedom. He was bringing his girls home and even using the double bed. His mind was stuck on one issue and it played over and over all day long. He wanted to be the first with his daughter. He was on his way when she started screaming in the bedroom. Now, if he could find her, he would have her all to himself.

He put out the word to friends and foes that his wife and daughter were missing and he offered a large reward for information. He felt like making that end bit say 'dead or alive', but thought better of that.

Thomas woke on the Saturday a week into the plan to loud knocking. He grumbled and threw on a pair of shorts and a T-shirt. He opened the door to two rough looking characters, rather unkempt.

"What's all the racket for?"

"We know where your missing persons are hold-up. We've come to collect the reward and tell you their whereabouts."

"Not so fast gentlemen. It reads, you tell me first; I check out the information and if correct I pay, got it?"

"Sorry mate but we get paid first then tell you where they are camped out."

"I'll tell you what. I'll pay you 20% of the £1000 then you give me the location. If I believe it is possible then I give you another 20%. After that nothing until the two runaways are back here. How's that for being fair?"

The two strangers were frowning as they worked the figures. "Okay we'll accept your offer of £400. They were sighted in Melbourne yesterday getting off a tram near Victoria Station. Now that's £200 quid mate."

Thomas closed the door and called out, "That's useless information so get out of here."

Cursing, the two odd bods walked off punching each other on the shoulders. "They must think I'm thick, Melbourne indeed those two are too scared to even walk over the Bridge by themselves. No, they are in Mildura somewhere staying with one of their relations."

◦○◦

Matty had the plan moving along as quickly as he could. He was excited to believe that he was getting two women for the price of one. Edna would be behoven to him for rescuing her from domestic violence. All those bashings she described to him were shocking. As for Joy a few weeks on the road and he planned to frighten her into his arms and maybe further. "I'll be her special angel, her saviour."

At the start of the final week Edna and Joy packed up ready to be taken to Robinvale, the next town east of Mildura. It was smaller than Mildura and was mainly a citrus and grape growing area. They would live in a hire caravan while putting the finishing touches to the caravan that Matty had been fixing up.

They would move all their belongings and shop for the essentials they would need as they travelled across Victoria. This was the scariest part of the plan as it wouldn't be difficult for someone to identify them or even worse for Thomas to be wandering around.

The plan was almost finished being applied and Joy was feeling hot and sweaty from all the scrubbing she had done in the caravan. The time was closing in on 7pm when she asked her mother if she could go to the communal showers for a quick refreshener. As there had been no sightings of Joy's father, Edna felt she would be safe. The showers were 30 yards away so a scream would be easily heard.

The shower was toasty warm and the jets covered the body in a light spray. Joy made all haste as she didn't want to be out of her mother's sight for any longer than necessary. Her hair was auburn and tinged with the red that was like her father's. Every time she looked at it she felt like pulling each strand of red out. She had wet it thoroughly and decided not to dry and brush it until she was back in the caravan. It was this decision that may have saved her life.

She picked up all of her belongings and pulled a long blue dress up and bolted for the door. As she came tearing out of the door way, she had to skip to the right to avoid a man who was walking briskly from her left. The movement happened in a second or two and as she charged on, she said a voluntary, "Oops, sorry," before continuing. When she reached the steps of the caravan, she suddenly was shocked to realise that the man she nearly bumped into was none other than Thomas Adams, her father.

Edna heard Joy scrambling into the caravan and breathing fast. She turned around in time to see her daughter throw herself into her arms and start to bawl. In between sobs she kept repeating, "It was him, it was him…."

They would never know whether her father recognised his own daughter. Maybe it was the wet straggly hair that left him doubting who the young teenager was, who came rushing from the communal showers.

They were certain that he didn't do any of the threatened things he told them he was going to do when he found them. Then again it was Matty who continuously fed these threats to them. He had them firmly in his grip and while he kept up the belief that he was their saviour and protector then they needed him.

The very next day Matty came by. After hearing Joy's story of nearly running into her father, he packed up and hitched the caravan to the car. He insisted the two ladies get in the car immediately.

Once all was settled he drove out onto the highway and accelerated. He had to get the three of them out of harm's way.

One of the questions he asked Joy numerous times was, "Did he have a shot gun? The word around Mildura was he is hunting for us and has bought a shotgun and bullets."

They drove hard and fast all day. Along bitumen and then turning off onto gravel tracks. To the south then east and back north or whatever. He kept up a constant chatter that was a scare tactic. For Joy it worked to the point where she was sobbing.

Matty stopped the car in thick bush and sat in the back seat and cuddled the young girl until she settled. Their lunch was eaten in the car and drinks followed the same path.

Matty was making sure that the two women were scared out of their wits. "He could be anywhere along this road or have his spies waiting behind a bush or corner. We need to stay vigilant and pressing on as far away as possible before someone recognises us."

Matty pushed the car until six o'clock then he slowed and seeing a sign with Swan Hill on it turned off to the right along a bush track. Logically one would turn off on the side one is travelling on. So, to create a false trail Matty turned the opposite way.

They left the caravan hitched in case of an emergency exit, had a cold dinner and bedded down for the night. Matty was keeping the pretence of the boogie man is following so he told the girls he would take first watch. At 12 pm he would change with Edna and at 6am Joy would have her turn.

Chapter 29

After the change over with Edna, Matty was pleased to find Joy in the caravan bed. He quietly snuggled in while Joy slept after her tiring day keeping watch out for her murderous father.

Early in the morning they were packed and, on the road. Matty had slowed as he was concerned about the fuel. "The faster you go the more petrol you use," he told the passengers.

The trio reached the Havelock Crossing and panic set in when they had to stop for a train to go through. It felt like an eternity to Joy who nearly twisted her neck out of joint.

The town of Eddington loomed in front of the runaways and Matty stopped for a quick run to the newsagent. He returned with a newspaper and a note book. He threw the Reporter's Note book into the back seat followed by a blue biro and said to Joy, "Here this can be your diary of your trip across Victoria."

Joy opened the book and on the first page in her best swirling writing wrote Trip Book 1955. On the right-hand side in small letters was the beginning, "My house from April 24th."

They were nearing Bendigo when Joy wrote about seeing the mountains on both sides of the highway and was impressed by the greenery of the area. At 4.30pm they reached the gold centre of Bendigo.

They drove over the Campaspe River Bridge. Due to flood waters from the river they had to carefully drive the 'good old holden' slowly. Joy sat quietly in the back seat and kept her fingers crossed. All went well and they were once again on the open road then accelerating towards Stanhope.

As they passed through Murray Groves, they called into a packing shed and Matty asked the manager if there was any work. As he explained to the girls they would need to find jobs on the way so as to keep enough food on the table. The manager said no but if they were to go on to Daylesford they might find a few small towns along the way and Joy wrote these in her new diary. Byrneside and Mooroopna flashed by before the city like buildings of Shepparton seem to rise out of the plain. No stopping in this large town so onward Matty drove through Numurkah, Katanga, Strathmerton, Yarroweyah, Cobram, Toccumal, Mulwalal, Yarrawonga and onto Albury.

Joy was still nervous about the trip and the need to get away from her father. Both her mother and Matty kept emphasising that Thomas could be anywhere and not necessary as himself. He had spies ready and willing to do what had to be done. This comment made Joy really concerned as she had already felt her father's method of getting his own way.

Odd though that her aunties had all been very receptive to Thomas and those rides by horse back over twenty miles in to town and then return over the same distance meant they were happy to be with him. She tried to imagine what they were getting up to as her knowledge of the male and female get togethers was limited through the protection of her mother. The relationship that Joy had built so quickly with Matty was evidence of her naivety as well as having a willing mentor in her mother.

At school her friends would talk about kissing with lips open wide and a tongue in the other person's mouth. "What was it they called this, oh yes French kissing".

One time another friend said her boyfriend lifted her dress to see what she wore underneath. Joy was shocked and her mother called the girl a filthy little hussy for allowing this to happen. To Joy her friend was wonderful so she probably didn't want that to happen and it was the boy who was smutty. Joy would continue to be protected by her mother for some years yet and even after she would be limited in her boy and girl knowledge.

Matty kept the car purring along and Joy wrote the towns in her diary as they passed through them.

Albury was the stopping post for the three tired people. A quick talk about staying in this city was followed by dinner in a mobile diner on the main street. The person serving was helpful in pointing out where the best caravan park was located.

The manager welcomed them all and even walked down to the lot they were to park the caravan in. He helped direct Matty into the correct space and to set up the electricity. They were all so tired that they virtually fell asleep at the first cosy place they found. Joy sat on a chair and nodded off. Matty flung himself on the double bed and his eyes glazed over in seconds. Edna laid on the bench that was around the table and she too fell into a deep sleep.

All three were startled awake by loud banging on the caravan door. Matty flew from the bed, grabbed the pick handle he kept ready for any intruders. Joy ran to her mother's side and hugged her.

"Whose there?" called Matty and waited for an answer. He was holding the pick handle like an American baseball player ready at home base to hit the pitch over the boundary.

"Sorry folks it's Bevan Cousins. I believe you are looking for work."

Matty let out a long sigh and tossed the handle onto the bed. 'I'll open the door."

The door was pushed open and the man who introduced himself as Bevan stood at the bottom of the steps, arm out-stretched.

"Mr Koch I believe," he said and shook Matty's hand. "Need two pickers for my potatoes just out of town. Ray from the take-away said you were looking for work and I'm desperate to get the potatoes boxed for market or they'll go rotten. Can't get a worker anywhere."

Matty accepted and Bevan gave him the directions. Bevan explained his manager would meet them just before they reached the house and get them settled in. The work would begin tomorrow with Edna and Matty boxing the potatoes and Joy becoming the Clean-up Manager for the caravan.

She would shortly get a job in the local cooperative behind the counter. This would prove to be longer term than the others. A fortnight in the potato paddock would be ten days' worth of wages for Matty and Edna.

Matty kept up the vigilance as lookout. He kept seeing Thomas or one of his henchmen. Every time he noted one or the other he was by himself. He would spin a scary story that made Joy tremble and Edna to go very quiet.

The latest sighting was of Thomas's red car parked outside the Albury Hotel. Matty had seen it in the evening while going to buy a bottle of lemonade from the Cafe. He had remained silent so he said as he didn't want anyone panicking. In the morning it was still in the same place when Matty went to buy the newspaper. Matty was most agitated when he arrived back at the caravan. He told the girls what he had seen while packing the gear and hitching the caravan to the holden.

"He's found us so we need to get away as fast as we can. It was definitely his red Cadillac parked outside the Albury Hotel. Our other option would be to go to the police but they won't do anything as there isn't enough evidence that Tommy has been involved in unlawful activities.

Joy didn't hesitate to clamber aboard the car although she kept up wanting to say goodbye to the friends she had made at the Co-op.

As the last thing the three had talked about was going to Mount Buffalo for work that was the way Matty headed. He pushed the car along until he reached Wangaratta. Here he turned off and took a minor road through Yackandandalga, to the highest mountain in the area. This was Mount Buffalo and somewhere here a farmer had a paddock full of potatoes ready to be pulled and washed.

Joy turned her window down and soon wound it back up. It was freezing. The trip up the winding road towards the summit was slow and scary. Joy was shaking by the time the car stopped. When she looked around she couldn't see a house nor a farm which confused her.

"Where's the farm and the paddock of potatoes?"

Matty spoke rather angrily, "They are further on. We have over heated the car and when that happens she stops. We have to sit this out until the engine cools so make yourselves comfortable.

A half an hour went by before a truck came from the road above them and stopped in front of the holden. A typical farmer stepped out and put a broad brimmed hat on his head. His overalls were muddy and the pair of rubber boots were also splashed with mud.

Matty opened the car door, shivered and walked to meet the arrival. "Hi mate, bloody cold. I'm Matty looking for a Harvey to help him pick potatoes for a week or two."

"I'm Vincent Harvey, the jobs just around the corner. Looks like you over heated the car. Towing a caravan up such a steep incline tends to do that. When you are ready drive another mile and park near the shed. You can hook into the electricity and set yourselves up. Hopefully the cloud will lift and we'll get a half day's work."

Vincent turned and walked back to his truck. After several three point turns he headed back up the mountain. Matty started the Holden's engine and followed. Harvey was right about the house, shed and potatoes in the field. Matty backed the caravan in and everyone helped get organised.

All three kept complaining of the cold and the slushy ground. Matty made the observation that he didn't think they would last a fortnight in this environment but they need to at least try.

The farmer, Vincent Harvey, arrived carrying two sets of weather proof coats, two pairs of rubber boots and two hats. "Right put these on and we'll get some of those spuds dug up."

Edna said, "Joy can help she may look small but she can work as energetically as the best."

The four workers were met at the gate of the potato paddock by three other workers. "Take a farrow each and work along filling up you sugar bag. When you get a full bag leave it in the farrow and start filling the next bag."

Edna, Joy and Matty worked solidly all afternoon and Vincent was pleased. The three were not so pleased with conditions and at tea in the caravan the negative comments gave way to a desire to pack up and leave. It was too cold, muddy, dirty and back breaking. They had not seen the sun all day and from the comments of their fellow workers they had not seen it either for over a week.

Matty disappeared up to the house and returned five minutes later with a bundle of notes in his hand. "We have been paid and we are now going back down off of this freezing mountain and continue our trip. Pack up while I put the £30 in the community bottle.

∾o∾

They made better time going down than coming up although the steep sides down to the valley were scary. Joy had to close her eyes and cross her fingers many times.

A few miles on their way back to Wangaratta Matty called out loudly, "Quick lock the doors and you two put your heads down."

There was such an urgency in his voice Edna and Joy pushed the window locking mechanism and flattened themselves on to the seat.

"It's Tommy's Cadillac coming up fast behind us. We've been found. Hopefully he won't recognise me or the caravan. Stay absolutely glued to the upholstery."

Matty continued to drive and give the girls a running commentary of what the other car was doing. It had cruised up behind and was sitting ten car lengths back. There was no intention noticed for the car to pass even though it had the engine power to do so.

The two cars reached the outer parts of Wangaratta and Matty said, "I'm going to stop outside the police station. This will get him off my bumper bar."

The two girls were still pinned to the seats and stayed that way even when the car stopped. A few minutes past and Matty said, "Well blow me down. The red Cadillac that was at the pub is still there and our follower has continued down the main street. You can look up."

They all sat in the car for over an hour watching to see if either of the two cars were on the move but nothing happened.

"I think you are wrong Matthew," said Edna. "Can we go on to Albury now?"

Matty reversed out onto the main road and sedately drove off along the main street.

∽o∾

An hour later they were driving through Albury. Matty stopped in the centre of the double city of Albury-Wodonga and asked for directions. Edna had friends in the town and there was the hope that Joy could stay with them for a long break and even work at the local co-operative Ltd.

This was easily arranged once they found Val and Peter, Edna's old school mates.

Joy said a teary goodbye to her mother and Matty as they were going south towards Melbourne. The rest of the plan depended on how long they were away for. As it happened they arrived back in Albury-Wodonga almost on the sixth month.

∽o∾

Joy was overjoyed to see them again and upset because she was about to leave her friends from Albury-Wodonga. She climbed in the back seat and away they went, all hands waving and lots of goodbyes.

Joy called from the back seat, "There's the road to Gundagai to our right. Can we go and see the Dog and the Tucker box?"

"That's a clever idea," said Matty.

The towns with impossible to spell names flashed past and Joy wrote these in her diary; Bowna, Woomargama, Holbrook, Tarcutta, Tumblay and then there was Gundagai.

Chapter 30

The journey from Albury was devoid of scares and red cadillacs so the three were feeling a lot happier. Towns like Bowna, Woomargama, Holbrook, Tarcutta and Tumblay flashed past. Nothing untoward happened although every red car and caravan caused panic attacks.

Photographs of the dog and one with each of the travellers was followed by an icecream.

They found a caravan park in Gundagai. All three settled in and all fell fast asleep quickly.

Unfortunately, no one had the sense to lock the car back door.

The driver of the red Cadillac had smiled broadly when he watched the little blue caravan pull out from the side road and onto the Wangaratta Highway. He reached over and felt the stock of the shot gun under the blanket. "Five thousand pound will be so easy to get and spend, but twenty thousand alive is a more lucrative reward. The kid's a skinny lightweight so it shouldn't be too hard to grab and run. Then again if

I can separate her from the other two I'd be home," he thought.

He had followed the caravan all the way in and believed the driver was unaware of him. He drove on past the police station to at least take some of the vigilance way. Now he sat well off the road waiting for the caravan to pass by. Sure enough almost on the hour the caravan sped past. The driver pushed his fingers through the receding, auburn hair and started the motor. The caravan would most likely be headed for the Dog on the Tuckerbox in Gundagai as it was a favourite of the youngest person in the holden.

By the time Matty had the holden parked near the Dog on the Tucker-box the red Cadillac had pulled up at the back of the cafe just down the main street from the famous sculpture. The man leaning on the driver's door was unknown to Matty and Edna. Neither spoke to Joy about the red Cadillac as they didn't want to scare her. The trio took several photographs and then Matty said, "Everyone hop in and we'll find a caravan park for the night."

Edna and Joy clambered in the holden but Matty stayed outside on the passenger side. He indicated to Edna to wind down her window. "I'll have a word with our spy and see what he's up to."

'I doubt he would do anything stupid in the main street. If he does start something shuffle across to the driver's seat and high tail it to the police station that you can see a couple of hundred yards further on."

Edna was not pleased with the turn of events and began to beg Matty to get in the car.

He ignored her and set off across the road. The man beside the Cadillac took a cigarette from his lips and flicked it on to the bitumen. He crushed it with his right foot and began walking towards the cafe door. Matty met him before he entered and from where Edna was seated she made out a greeting followed by a short conversation before Matty returned to the car.

He opened the driver's door and got behind the wheel. Edna handed him the keys while asking, "Who was he and what did he want?"

"I introduced myself and asked if he knew of any work around the town. He says he is a local by name of Evan Byers and has a farm out of town. No work is available as far as he knew. He offered me good luck and went inside. The Cadillac is not Tommy's as the number plate is wrong."

The night at the caravan park left the three travellers skittish and even though they were satisfied that Evan Byers was not a threat to them they couldn't get it out of their heads how easy it could be for someone evil to do something to any one of them.

∽⚬∾

In the morning Edna rose first and dressed. She went outside to see where the showers and toilets were located as they didn't bother to wash last night due to the fact that they were all weary and shaken up.

No sooner had she walked a few steps and then turned to come back to the caravan she cried out for Matty. "Matty come and see this quickly. Someone has written a message on the side of the caravan."

Matty came flying down the steps partly dressed and trying to pull his trousers up above his knees. "What, where, oh hell no, so it had to be our Mr Evan Byers on behalf of one, Thomas Adams. Cowardly little prick."

From behind came a shrill scream and Joy shouted, "Who is coming to get me, mum?"

Edna ran to her and gave her a long tight hug. "No, my dear not you. We need to get to the police as soon as possible and also tell the manager of the caravan park what has happened."

"I have to leave the message on the caravan for all to see. Get packed up and we'll get moving pronto," said Matty.

Joy said, "I'll write down what that man wrote on the caravan in my diary. She ran for the back seat of the car, grabbed her book and biro and wrote. 'Here to get Joy.'

The police sergeant was shocked and very concerned after hearing the story from the three runaways and inspecting the writing on the caravan.

"I have your statements and will telephone Mildura shortly and get them to investigate Mr Adams. He had better have proof of his whereabouts over the past week. As for using another standover merchant I'll get them to locate and interrogate all of his acquaintances. This sort of unlawful nonsense will not be tolerated."

Matty, Edna and Joy trooped from the police station after assuring the sergeant they would check in each morning and afternoon to leave there whereabouts and if any odd happenings are noted. The sergeant agreed to telephone through to nearby towns and towns on the trio's trip and alert them to the incident.

Matty drove the car and caravan to the nearest petrol station and got the mechanics to wash off the threatening message. Luckily the writing was in water colour paint and easily scrubbed off. Matty thanked the mechanic and paid him for his troubles.

"Sorry about this Mr Koch but people around here are usually very well behaved I'm sure the police will catch the culprits."

The touring party drove into Cootamundra and began searching for a caravan park. It wasn't long before one of the locals who Matty had pulled up near to pointed out where to find the Leisure and Pleasure Caravan Park. The three travellers were met by a bubbly middle-aged woman who explained the rules and set up the electricity for the caravan. She accepted the three pound from Matty for the one night and cheerily said, "Best of luck and enjoy your stay."

Within minutes of settling in a police car pulled up and Constable Raymond wound down the window and introduced himself. "Hear you are having some problems so I'll keep an eye out for any trouble. Here's my card if you need to telephone me at any time."

Matty said thanks and the policeman drove away.

"Can't believe how on the ball these coppers are." said Matty.

All the excitement and stress had left Matty desiring a night with Edna so he sent Joy to the car with a rug and pillow. She was happy to go as at times the noises and rocking in the caravan were annoying.

Chapter 31

Joy was soon settled and she fell into a deep sleep. Neither Matty or Joy had locked the left hand back door.

From his hiding place outside of the caravan park a man dressed in dark blue jeans and a black cardigan watched excited. "These idiots are playing into the trap," he observed. He adjusted the cap he was wearing and pushed up to the tree he was sitting against.

He had left all the weapons he had at his house as he didn't want the girl hurt as the higher price was enticing. All he had to do was wait for the caravan park lights to be switched off at 10.30pm then run doubled over to the car where he had seen the girl enter with her rug and pillow. A few squirts from the plastic bottle full of ether and that would keep her sleeping.

She was a light-weight so fireman's carry over the shoulder back to the car that was parked a couple of hundred yards away. Once he was home he needed to ring the money man to collect and twenty grand was his.

When he thought of the times he was so close to nabbing the kid he couldn't believe the interruptions to his plans. He was recruited along with six others back in the Mildura Hotel by Thomas Adams.

∽o∾

Adams was talking loud and boasting about the number of young girls he had the pleasure of their company in the past ten years. The men standing around in the lounge with a free beer in their hand all knew he was a philanderer. They also knew him as a man who threw his money around loosely.

Thomas called the men to attention and outlined his need of them, emphasizing the reward. The ears of each pricked up at the £20 000 on offer to simply catch a young girl and return her to Thomas.

Thomas took out a photograph and held it up for all to see. The young girl was a beauty and they knew what the speaker wanted with her. "How old is she Thomas?" asked Jack Newton a local citrus fruit farmer. He was there for the money because his land was too small to make a proper living. The oranges he picked each year gave him just enough to exist until the following harvest.

"She's my daughter, Jack and I have every right to have her returned to the family home. Her mother has taken her against her will and I want her back. Her three brothers are missing her and want her returned as well. As for the mother she can rot in hell."

No one else asked questions as the force and anger in Thomas's voice warned them off. As he was speaking he moved among the six men and handed them a photograph so they knew what this youngster looked like.

The crowd broke up and as they were leaving the lounge area Garry Ibson nudged Sam McFarlane and whispered, "Not his type really her breasts are too tiny."

"I agree," said Garry , then added, "She turns sixteen in November and he wants to be at the front of the line. Poor kid having a father like that. If I find the girl I won't be in a hurry to bring her in."

Bob Athwaite left quickly through the main swinging doors. He had a long drive back to his home town of Wangaratta. He believed that the bloke who was travelling with Thomas's missus and daughter would head for Sydney and more than likely pass through Albury within the next few days. He certainly hadn't anticipated six months. Any how they were now here and his plan was working too well.

He was rather shocked when the bloke with the young Adam's girl came up to him at the café this afternoon. He only asked about work so maybe he genuinely knew nothing about what Bob was up to nor that he was working with Tommy Adams. He settled down in the driver's seat on the far side of the Gundagai Caravan Park. It was 10 pm, not long to wait now. At 10.20 pm he made a move towards the caravan, stopped by a tree and sat down.

The Caravan Park lights went out.

It took Bob Athwaite several minutes to adjust his eyes to night vision and another couple to stand up and stretch his aching muscles. "Must be getting old," he thought out loud. He lifted the spray bottle full of ether, shook it to make sure there was plenty of the liquid available. According to his reading, three squirts should knock the kid out for two hours. She would be all trussed up and sleeping in one of the beds back at his place in Wangaratta by that time.

Bob climbed over the Caravan Park fence and made a bee line for the holden and caravan. He stopped to check his surroundings and to ensure there was no one moving around. All clear so he hurried on.

He moved directly to the back left door of the car and lifted the handle and it opened. At the same moment there was movement in the caravan and soft moaning. He laughed at the dichotomy, "the two inside the caravan were enjoying life but the little one in the car was about to be kidnapped."

Bob opened the door quarter of the way and peered in. The girl Thomas had called Joy was sleeping with her head on the other side of the back seat, Bob pulled the door wider open and keeping the spray ready eased himself towards her head. He didn't want to get too close as the spray would wet her and wake her up. She no doubt would start screaming and the game would be up.

Bob took a large gulp of air through his mouth and pressed the spray trigger three times, aiming the liquid in the air towards the sleeping girl.

A few seconds went by and all seemed to be working as he envisaged. Suddenly she coughed and Bob flew backwards out of the car. He landed on his backside and stayed stock still. Nothing else moved. The car door was now wide open so he moved back and touched the youngster on the nose.

Nothing.

He squeezed the nose lightly and again nothing happened. She should be out to it by now. He decided to risk the move and swept her up in his arms and partly dragging and lifting got her out of the car. Her threw her roughly over his shoulder and set off at a jog towards where he had left his car.

Constable Mainwaring of the Gundagai police had been on duty since 1200 hours and felt something was wrong. It was one of those feelings you couldn't explain but as a copper he usually found that it had some truth to it. People in the force talked about 'Go with your gut'.

Mainwaring was tossing up between making another coffee or going for a drive around the town. It would be his sixth coffee since he ate dinner at 1800 hours. He stood up and walked towards the coffee jug and kept walking. The gut feeling had won out.

He drove down the main street and turned towards the river. As he approached the bridge, he saw a car parked well off the road facing away from town. Two things alerted him to a feeling that this wasn't normal. A car that had broken down or run out of petrol would not have been parked well off the road. The driver would have tried to make as much distance as possible towards a house ahead to get help.

He stopped the police car across from the other car and went to check if anyone was around. Nothing was moving and there was no evidence of anyone trying to fix a broken-down car.

A flat tyre usually would show signs of a jack being used with scuff marks where the jack is placed. Signs that the spare tyre had been dragged from the boot and rolled along the sand and so on. The most concerning thing was the hood was hot in fact too hot for a local car. This car was driven at speed for quite a long way and here it was parked well off the road.

Constable Mainwaring was looking towards the bridge looking out for any house lights ahead where someone may have gone for help when the lights of the Caravan Park went out.

"Must be ten thirty," he mumbled to himself. He walked back to the police car to radio his position in and what he was investigating. He asked the telephonist who was manning the radio to give him ten minutes to check out a few things and if he wasn't in touch to send out another car to assist.

Constable Mainwaring walked along the left-hand side of the road to go over the bridge. He travelled fifty yards past the bridge and turned to cross the road and move back to his car. He was surprised to see a light shining from the first pole of the bridge. It was like a torch or a lantern. He moved quickly to check out what was creating the light. It was indeed a small torch stuck with tape on the pole and facing on an angle into the bush. This immediately alerted the policeman that there was something afoot and it may need more than one person to deal with it.

The light had to be a signal or a positional marker for someone and the someone was possibly still nearby. Constable Mainwaring ran to the other side of the bridge and ducked down anticipating someone to emerge from the bushes and make for the torch. If he didn't call in, a car would be sent out shortly to help. He would try not to engage any one until the second car arrived.

The scene and the action started out normal but then it seemed to slow like a taped drama on slow motion. Constable Mainwaring heard the heavy footfalls coming from further along the road. They were sluggish and the person on the move was breathing heavily. He stayed in his place trying to calculate what he was about to face.

Bob Athwaite was not a fit man and as he headed for the bridge and the torch he had earlier planted, he knew it. The girl over his shoulder was a light weight and in his younger days would not have puffed him out.

He held the body tightly with his right hand and the spray bottle of ether was in his left. All of a sudden, a voice came from his right. A powerful torch stunned him and he stopped.

"Police, lower the bag and kneel on the ground."

The voice of authority stopped him in his tracks and he began to obey. The word police shocked him and he started to realise his game was up. The owner of the voice came towards him as he lowered Joy to the ground. He rose to his full height and his mind clicked back into the fight mode. He stepped towards the oncoming policeman and aimed the ether bottle at his face. He started pumping the ether into the face of the constable who was surprised by the attack.

Constable Mainwaring grappled with the man and spun him around creating a half Nelson. His training was snapping in as he grabbed his handcuffs from his belt and began to ready then to be snapped on the man's wrist. Everything began to slow down and his thinking was missing parts. He missed the wrist with the cuffs and found that he couldn't maintain his grip on the body of the man. His voice sounded distant and garbled. His knees buckled and he sunk to the ground.

Bob Athwaite turned to pick up the rug in which Joy was entombed. He was annoyed to find the body was missing. When he put her on the ground, he failed to notice a graded channel that led to the river. Joy had rolled about five yards away, and in the darkness, Bob couldn't locate her.

The sound of a siren split the still night as the backup police car came along main street. Bob was in panic mode and grabbed the torch attached to the bridge and ran as fast as he could to his parked car. He started the engine and spun the car 180-degree. With the lights off he accelerated over the bridge and beyond. He looked in the rear vision mirror but couldn't see the cop car with the siren blaring. He had to chance turning on his lights or he would run off the road.

The road ahead lit up and Bob floored the car and disappeared into the night. He had left the girl and the bottle of ether behind. Hopefully there were no other evidence to point to him.

Constable James Reid was in the backup car and as he neared the bridge he made out a body lying in the centre of the road not moving. It was Constable Mainwaring. Reid grabbed the radio mike and called, "Officer down. Send help and an ambulance."

The ambulance raced Constable Mainwaring away to the hospital. One of the paramedics ventured the diagnosis, "He's been drugged with ether, you can smell it over him."

It took a while to find Joy in the gutter. She also smelled of ether and was still fast asleep. Constable Reid placed her in the passenger back seat of his car and took her to the hospital. "We need to come back at first light to gather evidence to what appears to be a kidnapping and assault of an officer of the law. It's too dark to go hunting around in the bush and along the river. Whoever did this has gone."

It was 0610 when Matty threw his right leg over the edge of the bed and sat up. He dressed and went outside to wash the sleep out of his eyes and to clean his teeth. Edna was still snoring lightly in the double bed.

As he came down the steps he glanced towards the car and thought, "You're running out of time Matty boy. If you don't make a move pronto you'll miss out on her."

He stopped and looked at the right side back door. It was open. "How lucky can I be the chance may not have slipped by. She must be at the loo so I'll walk down and catch her in the shower block and tell her how much I love her."

At the showers he searched high and low and called her name but no response. He even had the silly notion that she may have mistaken the men's from the ladies'.

Despondently he wandered back to the caravan. He had got all excited all too soon and now he had to bring himself down out of the high or Edna might notice. He walked the long way around the park and came in from behind the van. Edna was sitting on a chair with her face in her hands.

Matty was about to speak when he heard police sirens and saw two cars tear through the entry of the park and pull up at the office. There was shouting and seconds later the two cars pulled up outside of Matty and Edna's van.

At the hospital, Joy had been aroused from her deep sleep and managed to tell the police who she was and that she was travelling with her mother and Matty. She gave them the location of the caravan and the names of her two touring mates.

One of the men who was in her room did not aappear to be a policeman as he was dressed in a dark blue suit. He carried a note book and constantly wrote notes. He did not join in asking the simple questions leaving these up to the uniformed police officers.

After nearly half an hour he nodded to the sergeant of the team and he ushered everyone from the room. The man in the suit introduced himself as Detective Brand and spoke very quietly. He explained that their was a person who was a danger to others and needed to be caught as quickly as possible. His questions were much more personal and deeper. At times Joy struggled to answer but the demeanour of the Detective was such that she knew of his urgency.

Detective Brand thanked Joy for her help and told her how brave she had been. He excused himself and went out the door. A swarm of hospital staff entered to check Joy's medical statistics and when satisfied they told the girl she could return to her mother.

One of the uniformed policeman was called and he explained that Joy could get dressed in her civilian clothes and that he would take her to the caravan park where her mother and Matty were awaiting her arrival.

Chapter 32

The police who went to the caravan park took most of the day to investigate the incident and to take copious notes for a file that seemed to get thicker by the minute. At about 1600 hours the Sergeant in charge, a Morris Gilmore called a stop and announced, "I think we have enough about what happened last night. We will let you and your young lady go on with your trip with our best wishes. If you or Joy recalls something report it."

The holden rolled out of the caravan park at 1615 hours with Joy fast asleep in the back seat. She knew nothing of her ordeal although she kept complaining of a bitter taste in her mouth. She had been feeling so tired all day now she could catch up on what she thought was lost sleep.

Matty was in a research role trying to figure out what had happened and if the bloke who tried to snatch Joy was alone wolf or a member of a gang. The latter he was siding with the gang being led by Thomas C. Adams.

While he analysed this and that aloud Edna was more circumspective and was so relieved that they had found Joy and everything was almost back to normal.

"You know," said Matty, "I feel that there was something afoot the day we saw the red Cadillac on the highway. I know the number plates of that one and the other we saw at the petrol station and that neither matched Thomas's but all the same. If I had pressed that bloke at the garage, I could have averted all of the dramas we have all been through...." His voice droned on and Edna closed her eyes for a nap. She awoke as Matty pulled into the Canberra Caravan Park.

The manager, a young lady maybe nearly thirties, bustled out with a large ring of keys swinging in her right hand. "One caravan £3 and for electricity another £1 for one night. Staying longer? No then follow me to lot 66 and I'll leave you to set up."

It took until 2100 hours before Joy opened her eyes and looked around. She was inside the caravan laying on her back. The horrid dream she had just woken from wasn't real thank goodness for that. She became aware of Matty and her mother. Her eyes flicked to the 12-hour clock that was attached to the wall above the sink. She wasn't sure it showed morning or afternoon.

"Hello my love," said Edna turning to face her. She and Matty had been playing cards and Edna still had five cards in her hand. "Are you feeling better after all you have been through."

Joy looked at her mother and asked, "What have I been through? I feel really rested and the last thing I remember was shutting the car door and snuggling down in the back seat."

"Leave well alone," chipped in Matty, "I did say she wouldn't recall anything. It is probably better she not know. Tomorrow we will be driving into the city of Sydney. We will be staying at a place called Yass because one of the para medics who was here last night said we would be able to get work there. He mentioned a caravan park so work and home will be close together."

Joy looked quizzically and asked, "Paramedic, like an ambulance driver. Why was he here last night?"

Matty provided the answer. "He was up by the office when I ran in to him. Lovely chap and very talkative. Wanted to know where we'd come from and where we were going."

"I hope you didn't tell him our secrets as he might be working for Thomas. I wouldn't like to be kidnapped you know, said Joy. Edna and Matty exchanged furtive looks. "Don't worry you're safe my dear," assured Edna.

∞

The next day Matty planned and executed a sightseeing visit to Canberra. He drove the girls around the roads that were all circular to many well-known places. They marvelled at Lake Burley Griffin, Parliament House where the politicians run the country, King George V Shrine, National Art Gallery and the huge War Memorial.

∽o∽

While the trio from Mildura relaxed in Canberra, Max had been thumbing a lift all the way from Tamworth in little moves and was getting tired. He was now in a Mac with a huge, jovial man of six feet six . "My name is Eddy what's yours? Where you headed matey?" he boomed above the truck's engine noise.

"Just call me Max J. Bound for Sydney and a new life, "said Max.

"Max, that rings a bell. My boss often talks about his brother Max. Apparently the brother was a mechanic for the business but one day he disappeared. Just got up and vanished. The police did find parts of a human skeleton and determined that it was Max Johnson the boss's brother.

Max was taken aback by this news and went into survival mode. He didn't want anyone to know who he was and what he was up to. He had found the past eight years lonely and at times felt lost. Oddly this was his express intention when he rode away from the family all those year ago.

"Gee Eddy," he said, "that's a story and a half. My surname is Jenkins." He thought that would shut the truckie up and he'd forget all about the Max Jenkins he gave a ride to today.

Eddy was a talker so he continued on. "I'm headed for Wollongong so I'll pass through Parramatta in a few hours. Where would you like me to drop you off. If it's not out of my way by too long a shot I can put you down exactly."

"Mighty noble of you," said Max. "I'm headed for the mighty Panthers area," said Max.

"Penrith?" shouted Eddy, "Surely not. The only team worth following is the Rabbitos. I should put you out right here, but I won't."

The two had a common subject to talk about and argue about. Rugby League as it was called was a popular ball game in New South Wales and anyone in the state would debate the game and the teams. While the two talked and fought the truck licked up the miles.

The Mac began to slow and Eddy worked back through the gears. At cruising speed of eighty miles an hour the huge truck and its load of redwood was comfortable in tenth gear. Once in the city traffic Eddy had eased back to seventh gear. He was at times furious with the traffic around him.

"Bloody Sydney drivers," he kept saying and then pointing out the mistakes and near misses happening around him.

Now the truck was winding through the gears and the air brakes were pinging as Eddy prepared to bring the truck to a stop.

Max said his thank you and goodbye as he stepped down from the truck. "It's been a pleasure meeting and travelling with you." He slammed the door and stepped back. As the truck roared away Eddy blew his horn long and friendly. He would kick himself in a week's time when he got back to the depot.

Max picked up his swag and began to walk to the petrol station he could see across a barren paddock. He needed somewhere to stay and a good meal. The owner of the garage suggested he try the café a few blocks away for the meal and then he could walk to the Parramatta Caravan Park where his van was waiting. Max thanked the man for the information and set off on his search.

Since leaving the family in an angry state he had roamed from here to there always using an alias. He had a few foul episodes with people and some loving ones as well. He now was settled at Parramatta with a steady job working for Bilney Roadworks Co a road repair company. He also had a girlfriend, Danielle who he hoped to catch up with in the next 24 hours.

Unfortunately, he was facing a bit of bad luck as he had been informed that the Parramatta Caravan

Park was about to close and he had to find another. The Parramatta manager was kind enough to suggest the Blacktown Caravan Park a couple of miles away.

Max found the new park easier enough and he paid the manager for one week. The manager pointed to a rundown van and said, "All yours mate. Do a few jobs around the outside and inside and it'll go from a man's humpy to a king's castle." He laughed at his own joke and wandered off.

Max was pleased with the rental charge of 2/- a day but the van was in need of a full renovation. The surrounds were full of rubbish and parts of cars. From his position he could count four bald tyres and he couldn't see the other side as yet.

Inside the damage and mess was worse. The simple solution was to find a broom and sweep the whole lot out the door, pick up the pile and deposit all the rubbish in the 44-gallon drum that was nearby. By midafternoon he had a bare interior but it was clean. The surrounds would have to wait.

Many of the other caravans in the park were in similar mess as his so he didn't stand out.

∽o∽

Matty, Edna and Joy were enjoying their drive into the city of Sydney. They arrived at the St Clair's Caravan Park at 1300 hours feeling peckish. The owner was pleased to have their patronage. He helped set up and directed them to a diner for a meal.

While eating a hamburger and cheese with tomato sauce liberally squirted over, they began discussing the prospect of work.

The waitress came and went a few times to assure they were happy with their meal and to offer further food from the menu. She plied them with anything they asked for. When they were finished the waitress approached and began clearing the dishes they had used. She stopped part way through the clearing and said, "Sorry, but I couldn't help but hear parts of your conversation. We have a job going here for a young girl and it pays 50p a day. Your young daughter could do that with my support. What do you think?"

Joy looked around at the neat café and the limited menu and was happy to agree. The waitress turned out to be the co-owner of the business.

Matty and Edna left Joy at the cafe and drove back to the Caravan Park. It was now up to them to find their jobs so they could contribute to the communal pot.

Sydney was a bustling, noisy and rushed city. The trio found that catching the train system was the cheapest and easiest way to travel.

Each weekend they would map out a place at the end of the rail system and go for a ride to have a look around. Within a couple of months, they were conversant with the layout of the city, Matty had found a job working in mining talc and Edna was serving in a hotel.

Max Jenkins, as he told Eddy the truckie, was still at Blacktown Caravan Park watching the World go by. Every morning he awoke at 0600 hours, sat up and pulled the curtains across letting in the sunlight. His view was a bare patch of gravel with a wooden sign Blacktown Caravan Park, and further away was a road then the pastures of a dairy farm. Most mornings a dozen cows would be grazing the lush green grass.

Max would stretch, roll out of bed and check his calendar to see if he had any appointments. On week days he was off to work as a steam roller driver for the Bilney Road Works Company. He was a valued worker as his mechanics skills were invaluable to the company, that had a catch phrase, "If it wouldn't start then call Max and he'd have it on the move within half an hour."

On weekends he would walk miles keeping fit and looking at the city views. He had been a country boy all his life so he was mesmerised by the sky scrapers and of course the 'coat hanger' as the locals called the Sydney Harbour Bridge.

One morning Matty, Edna and Joy were sitting in their caravan when there was a knock at the door. Upon opening the door they found the manager who told them she had bad news. The park was closing at the end of the week due to lack of customers and the property sold. The new owners were interested in using the land for growing vegetables for the Sydney market. With apologies all around the manager advised the three that they must vacate by Thursday. He recommended another caravan park that was a couple of miles towards the city at St Blair's. He produced a map and pointed out where it was and how to get there.

Although they had only been at St Blair's for half a year it was rather sad to have to uproot themselves and move on. They found the area peaceful and had not been harried by Thomas and friends since the kidnapping. The court case that Matty and Edna were privy to and sent the daily outcomes, had seen Bob Aihwaite sentenced to ten years in gaol. This had knocked the wind out of Thomas's desires. Joy appeared to be safe.

Joy was not aware of the story and her place in

it. One day soon after the court case had begun in Albury, Joy had come home carrying the newspaper. It was her responsibility to buy the paper after her work shift and bring it for Matty to read. Joy was quite excited by the time she walked through the Parramatta Caravan gates. As she handed the paper to an expecting Matty she said, "Did you know about the kidnapping at Albury? A young girl my age was grabbed from a caravan and taken during the night. Luckily a policeman found the man carrying the girl and arrested him. Boy I'm glad that it wasn't me!"

Matty looked at Edna and said, "We wouldn't let anyone harm you Joy, you are safe with us." He then turned the paper to page 2 and started reading. It was at this time no one was allowed to disturb him so the kidnapping news had been dealt with.

The move from Parramatta was without any dramas except that it was done in the middle of the night. The caravan was packed by mid-day and hitched to the tow ball of the holden. All they had to wait for was the new manager arriving to check them out. This entailed inspecting the caravan lot, all rubbish had been cleared and the final payment of £11 collected. The keys to the electricity had to be returned and the release form signed by both parties.

All straightforward and simple or so they thought. The retiring manager had inspected the site at two in the afternoon and told Matty that the new owner was having car trouble and would be a couple of hours. As it turned out 'the longest two hours ever' quipped Matty when the papers were finally signed at ten past midnight.

The trio set off to a caravan park in St Mary's and when they arrived all was locked and barred. Matty in his frustration took the gate off its hinges and drove in to park at the first vacant lot. They were lucky to find the electricity had been unlocked so at least they were able to see.

Noting that there were several other vans at the park they kept their noise level to a minimum and got to sleep at one o'clock.

Joy made an observation about the caravan that was nearby where they had set up. "Whoever lives in that van must be spooky and dirty. Just look at how untidy it is all around and he's a bikie."

Edna said, "Hush, my dear he could be a lovely man you must never judge people until you meet them. Go to sleep. We'll need an early start to unpack everything and do the washing."

At six o'clock in the morning Max awoke and pulled the curtains across to look out the window. He blinked several times before realising his view was blocked by a little rounded blue caravan. He was not impressed as the new arrival had spoilt his view.

As he sat there pondering who these new people were and how he could convince them to move to another sight he saw was an angel descend the steps of the blue van carrying a wicker basket full of wet clothes.

The young figure took Max's breath away and he watched in awe as the girl walked to a rope that had been set up between the electricity pole and the caravan as a make-shift clothes line.

Chapter 33

The slim figure was wearing a short yellow cotton dress and as she bent to place the basket on the ground. Max was sure he caught sight of the white of her knickers. He couldn't believe his luck and started to believe he'd been sent to heaven.

The young girl unwittingly continued to excite Max who felt he should have more manners than perving on a beautiful girl. Try as he might he could not drag himself away from the bobbing girl and the movement of the yellow dress. The occasional flash of white was exciting to say the least.

The final dolly peg was put in place to hold a pair of men's blue trousers before the girl turned and walked back to the van. Max was by now hallucinating and couldn't tell reality from fantasy. He was sure that at the top of the steps the young lady turned her head towards him and gave a little wave.

She disappeared inside. He was breathless and had to remain still for some time. He waited expectantly for a return but nothing else stirred.

Max looked along the clothes line and in his reckoning could make out a woman's wardrobe and a man's clothes and of course a young girl's. Three people most likely mother, father and daughter.

Max dressed and shaved. He added Brylcream to his hair and combed it flat with a part on the left.

While he was preparing to look presentable, he had placed two slices of bread in the toaster. He spread one with vegemite and the other with orange marmalade. He ate fast with the intention to go over and introduce himself to the new comers. He was especially anxious to say hello to the daughter.

The lines that were drawn from corner to corner indicated the days he would be camped away. The date today was 4th November and the cross outs finished on 22nd February next year. Max sat down despondent and started counting all the crossed days.

∽o∾

Joy had a boyfriend of sorts in that they had met once in Mildura and gone to the movies together. She had written to him twice a year for the past three years. She signed the beginning, 'To my Graham' and finished with lots of kisses even though she had never kissed him. It was more of a fantasy relationship rather than real. He was happy to play along but the truth be known he had a girl who he was extra close to. With this young lady he held hands, kissed and went out together.

Matty read Graham's letters when they arrived and Joy's replies. One evening after the latest letter had been opened and read, he turned to Edna and whispered, "Joy is going to get hurt with this one I think she should write back and end the relationship."

Edna thought for a while and hoping that her gut feeling was wrong nodded in agreeance. Matty spoke to Joy for some time about falling in love with boys and the need to have a long courtship so you get to know your boyfriend in every possible way. He suggested she write to Graham and tell him she was too far away now to pursue a courtship with him.

It was to be a polite but serious letter. Joy started writing and would ask for help with the spelling. Matty seemed to Edna to be enjoying the letter writing and she wondered why?

Edna listened with some intrepidation as she could feel in Matty's voice an ownership of her. She often wondered why Matty acted as a protector of Joy and gave her advice that kept her within reach. Did he have a 'thing' for her. She wasn't concerned about what he thought of her as he had already repaid her a thousand times over by taking her away from a violent and violating relationship with Thomas. He showed all the wonders of physical contact and told her constantly how much he loved her.

There were times when Edna had heard similar words from Matty to Joy. He had worked the running away from a monster story in such a way that Joy would rush into Matty's arms without hesitation.

Most of the times while they were escaping Matty would set up the caravan in the most conspicuous places and left the caravan unhooked. One would have expected that for a fast get away the caravan would he hooked up and ready to fire. At one place Matty even placed pot plants around the camp site.

The show of being the saviour was evident in Matty's demeanour. Of course, there were other things he could have been doing but did not show or was it his smart ability to cover-up. He could have invited Joy into the caravan where he could see her in her nightie, or sharing the bed all three, or accompanying her to the showers in pretence of keeping her safe, or touching certain places on her body when they were cuddling or even making his kisses passionate.

Matty had finished his talk about breaking it off with Graham and Joy had accepted the idea. She took out a pad and biro and begun writing. Five minutes later and some tears she handed her effort to Matty who nodded sagely as he read through the letter. Edna accepted the letter and read it. She was still having second thoughts when Matty jumped up and snatched the letter from her hands and told Joy to address an envelope and stick a stamp on it.

"That deals with that problem," he said cooly. "Bedtime for all of us. Joy you can sleep in the caravan with us tonight. If you care to, you are welcome to sleep in the middle of the two of us."

Edna looked at Matty who had a wry smile on his face and opened her mouth to protest but froze at that position. The whole plan had been Matty's from beginning to now and she could only be thankful for little mercies in being saved. Maybe Matty needed rewards from Joy as well considering what her father had in stall for the girl if Matty hadn't helped.

Matty made overtures from that time onwards that placed Joy in easy physical reach. He was cunning and careful enough to make his nonconsensual advances as loving and to have Joy show delight when they occurred. Unknowingly Joy enjoyed the attention of the new Matty. For Edna it was as the saying said, 'Keep your friends close and enemies closer.' For Edna it was 'Keep Joy close and Matty even closer'.

∞◊∞

Three months is a long time and Max was beside himself thinking about the beautiful young lady he had seen at the St Marys Caravan Park. Would she still be there when he got back, would she and her parents accept him as a friend and then a lover of their daughter and did she already have a boy? So many questions and all he had was a three-minute window to catch a glimpse of her.

Max was dropped off at the gate of the St Mary's Caravan Park and walked to the gate. He undid the latch and pushed the two parts open. He recalled this gate was lying on the ground when he left last November. The blue, round caravan was still standing where it had been when he walked past it three months ago.

The holden was parked near the caravan but there wasn't a soul around. His temptation was to knock on the door and introduce himself. That would be too presumptuous and may turn them off before he had a chance to be 'Mr Nice Guy'.

He went on to his own caravan and opened the door. The smell was like a blast from a rubbish dump and he made a mental note to clean the whole area up pronto. If the sweet little girl next door saw the rubbish in and around the lot she might be turned off before he got a chance to talk to her.

He put his swag on the bed and set to scrubbing the inside and then sweeping the outside surrounds. He was perspiring from the frenetic way he was working and knew he had to get to the showers before making any welcoming moves to the neighbours.

The shower was warm and plentiful and he scrubbed every inch of his body with a sweet-smelling cake of Lux soap. He dressed neatly with long grey trousers and a blue short sleeve shirt. Black leather shoes with tie-up shoelaces and grey socks completed the dressing. He found the lather, razor and shaving brush. While he lathered up using the brush he looked in the mirror to see a black, thick beard.

Max was guessing the couple and girl would prefer a shaved visitor than a bearded one. He rubbed the lather thickly over his face and the beard and began to carefully shave. Black hair cascaded from his face and soon the beard was removed. He wiped his face with a towel, gathered up his bag and walked off to his van. He was hoping that the family had returned and he could make his way and knock on their door.

Alas all was still locked so he went to his own van and lay on his bed. Within minutes he was fast asleep.

∽∘∼

Matty was the first one to notice that the area around the van next to theirs was swept clean and all of the rubbish was missing. "Good lord," he said, "It looks like Moses has returned. The flood must be over although I believe it has been more than forty days."

The trio had been out for the day and had caught the train at St Marys station and ridden all the way out to Richmond. They swapped trains at Blacktown. They had enjoyed a look around the historical area and the Macquarie Towns. They ordered lunch at a pretty café and caught the train back at three in the afternoon.

Max was awakened by the arrival of the family next door and rushed to the window. His heart missed a beat when he spied the young girl. She was far more beautiful than last he saw her. She looked more mature and grown a few inches taller. Now his dilemma was to rush out and introduce himself or wait agonising over the perfect time to visit.

He need not have despaired because Matty walked over and knocked on the door. Max answered and introduced himself. He thought about using an alias like the many times before but for some reason he felt he needed to be truthful. "Max Johnson," he said and pushed his right hand towards Matty. They shook hands and Matty said, "Come over and meet the family and you can tell us your story and we'll reciprocate."

Max was over the moon in being introduced to Joy and held on a little too long because she pulled her hand away. He said, "Hello," to Edna and accepted a glass of beer. He told his story first and it was straight forward in the telling. He went through his war experiences leaving out the parts that may have upset an innocent and lovely young girl.

He explained the complications in his family and what each member was likely to be doing at this time. He did not divulge that his trip from Brisbane had been nearly seven years in the making. He left out his failed marriage and his other girlfriend who was likely to pop in any time over the next week.

He did tell about his journey to the McPherson Ranges to find the Stinson aeroplane but left out the gory parts. He told them about his many hitch-hiking trips all over Queensland and New South Wales and the many road laying camps he had been working at over the years.

Matty took up the tale for the other two leaving out anything which might be taken negatively by this nice man who may be their neighbour for a long time. There was plenty of time to fill in the spaces if they found him to be honest and trusting.

Max had tried desperately to take a seat near to Joy as he found her like a magnet, oh so attracting. He wanted to know things about her then realised he was being too inquisitive. He decided to call it a day and with goodbyes echoing around he went off to his caravan.

All through the night Max kept waking up and easing the curtain open hoping to get a glimpse of the 17-year-old. Alas he was wasting his time.

The next day Joy was sitting on the steps of the caravan when a taxi pulled up outside the gate. An elderly couple was sitting in the backseat. The male was tall and dressed in a black suit. He alighted from the passenger side and helped the lady to step out. The man placed a hat on his head and offered the woman his elbow. She took a grip and together the two walked into the Caravan Park.

The manager came bustling over and stopped the two before they had advanced far in to the park. Joy couldn't hear the conversation but from the gesturing it appeared they were interested in next door's caravan. The manager left and the other two walked to Max's caravan and knocked on the door.

A sleepy looking Max opened the door and stepped back inside. Joy thought this odd as Max seemed frightened by the couple's sudden arrival. The male beckoned him to come out and so reluctantly he stepped down and the couple moved away a few yards.

A long conversation was held and then the lady stepped forward to give Max an embrace. The male shook his head and they, arm in arm, walked back to the waiting taxi.

They got in the back seat and the taxi drove away.

Max went back inside and closed the door. Joy was tempted to go over and knock on the door to see if he was feeling well. In the end she walked off to find her mother and relay to her what she had observed.

It was quite some time before Max brought the visit by the two elderly persons up in front of Matty, Edna and Joy. The group were enjoying a barbecue when the topic of parents came into the conversation. Matty was first explaining he didn't know all that much about his father who passed away when Matty was barely seven years old. His mother struggled with her two sons until she caught pneumonia. Three days in Mildura Hospital and she had died.

∽ᴑ∾

Edna talked about her father who started a cattle station after driving a herd of cattle from Adelaide to Werrimull. He was a hard working farmer but his heart failed at the young age of 42. Edna's mother who they all called 'Mother' continued to keep the station going with the help of her growing sons.

Joy wasn't asked to join in and Max had already heard her story from Matty.

Max was reluctant to talk about his father but did have some kind words about his mother who he called Marion. The family of ten had been close together as they grew into adulthood. Most were married and have children.

Joy interrupted and asked, "The two old people who came to your caravan a month back, were they your parents?"

Max replied in the affirmative and then shocked the group by explaining what they were doing here. "I was very surprised that they had found me because I tried to vanish after I was made to marry a young lady. The gossip around the area we lived in was that I was the father of her expecting baby. She claimed it was one of the Johnson boys. Well there are three of us and at the time of the accusation two were married. As I was the only single son my father pressured me to marry her. I had never been to bed with her so I wasn't guilty. My father wouldn't accept my pleas and then when mum insisted I had no choice.

"I ran off and left her and no one knew what happened to me. My eldest brother Burt runs a transport company that plies the east coast Melbourne to Brisbane. He never believed I was dead so he had his drivers look out and question people they mingled with. Someone got lucky and heard I was out here. After he told my father, my parents travelled by train all the way from Brisbane to Sydney to visit me. They felt it was considered imperative to see me as my mother was diagnosed with cancer and was dying.

"The elderly lady Joy saw was my mother and she wanted me to go back to Brisbane to help on the dairy as my father was getting on and would soon not to be able to cope. Considering how mean they had been to me, I refused. My mother gave me a hug and asked me to forgive her and my father for their treatment of me since I was nine years old. I agreed to forgive my mother but not my father. They then left and went back to Brisbane. My mother has since died and is buried in the Toowong Cemetery.

The old ute pulled up in a cloud of dust outside of Max's caravan on the next Wednesday. A young lady dressed like a rodeo rider jumped out and went to the caravan door and knocked vigorously and loudly. "Hey Maxie boy it's pig shooting time move your butt or we'll miss the party out at Tamworth."

Max opened the door and had his swag in his right hand and a 303 rifle in his left hand. He pulled the door shut and key locked it. He strode across to the neighbouring caravan and called out. "Matty I'm off shooting pigs. Will be away until tomorrow, can you keep an eye on things?"

Matty and Joy came around the corner and replied. "No problems Max. Best of luck." Joy hung back which disappointed Max.

The ute revved and the handbrake was released. And the driver spun a 180 degree turn on the loose gravel and took off through the gate. "Smart woman but she may cause an accident one day driving like a maniac," said Matty.

Max had every confidence in the driver as he had been with her many times. "You can slow down Danielle or the cops will pull you over. They were on the bend ahead yesterday." The driver took her foot off the accelerator and the car slowed.

"Where are we going today?" asked Max. Every pig hunt was to a different place and each was exciting. Feral pigs are the scourge of all the farmers over the ranges and the farmers encourage hunters to their properties to try and lower the numbers.

"O'Lochlan's," said Danielle. "The boys are waiting at the prickle bush thicket on the Bathurst Road. Then we have a four hour drive to O'Lachlan's. They own a spread before Dubbo. We've got seven shooters including myself so dad should get plenty of pork and bacon for his butcher's shop."

"Now tomorrow, from three o'clock, you've got me while the old man and mum dress the pigs we can use their bed," said Danielle.

Max knew her as a nymphomaniac and he had trouble keeping up with her desires. So far he has been able to be par although several offers were refused which created massive arguments. He knew she had a temper and was not one to get off-side.

They sped past the prickle bush thicket blowing the horn. Three holden FX model utilities came tearing out, dust flying and joined the convoy. It wasn't all that long before they came to a gate with O'Lachlan Farm: Sheep we keep but piggies we eat.

The convoy stopped inside the gate and a talk by Kevin, Danielle's brother was given to the six others. It was a warning about the danger of guns and the ferocity of tuskers who will chase rather than run away. Every one nodded and listened to the instructions.

The farm was over ten thousand acres and had a mountain range and forest running through a quarter of it. It was this unused part that contained the pigs. The owner was telling one of the boys that he counted forty pigs and piglets come out of the hills led by three old tuskers. So there were plenty to be had if you knew how to hunt and shoot accurately.

Max was ex-army and a crack shot. The boys fought over whose team he would be on. Danielle always won out as she was a driver and needed a crack shot to keep in the lead of the most pigs shot.

On the back of each ute was a steel frame for the shooter and spotter to stand. This gave them height to see the pigs and a sturdy place to rest the gun. The most important part played by this frame was giving the men on the back something to hold on to. If the driver has to stamp on the brakes the man on the back holds onto the frame and won't go flying over the bonnet.

The driver had to listen to the messages that were tapped through the cabin. One tap is forward, many urgent taps is stop.

It took half an hour to reach the foothills and look at the thick forest that grew on these. The object was to work in tandem with another ute. The first moved slowly fifty yards out from the edge of the clearing sounding the horn. The second ute came behind along the edge of the trees. The idea was to frighten the pigs and they tended to run for the open area which is easier to reach full speed on and the pigs can navigate to their favourite hiding place.

Within minutes a dozen piglets and a sow ran from the bush and crossed the path of the first ute. The shooter blasted away and at least three little pigs hit the dust.

An old tusker ran between the two cars squealing loudly and trying to call the female and piglets back. As they changed directions, they ran past car one straight into car two. The latter now had them all in the open. Max opened fire and kept pumping bullets into the animals.

The pandemonium ceased and the two cars pulled up beside each other. All the guns were left on the tray while the hunters jumped down and began to collect the carcases. They were working in the light of the two spotlights which only covered a 45 degrees arc.

Unknown to any of them the tusker that fell during the shooting was only concussed by a bullet that grazed his head. He staggered up and tried to balance on all four legs. He toppled over and waited. He struggled back up all the while getting angry and set to retaliate.

He finally felt able to run so he charged towards the gathering of humans. No one actually saw him coming in the darkness but when he appeared full speed breaking into the light all hell broke out.

There were screams of warning and men scattered in every direction. No one had a rifle and the only person in a position to attack back was Danielle.

She was sitting in the car behind the steering wheel and the engine was still ticking over. Ahead she saw and heard the men yelling and running. Suddenly she saw the tusker burst from the darkness headed directly for one of the shooters.

She slammed the clutch down and pulled the gear into the first and accelerated. She drove directly towards the pig. There were still two shooters between her and the tusker. She began pressing the horn and change into second gear. The yards diminished rapidly and she could see one of the escapers was in danger of being run over. She swung the car into a 180 degree turn just before the car and runner hit each other, the pig deviated around the car and focused on the man it had been chasing.

Meanwhile Max had sprinted to the back of the nearest ute and jumped onto the tray of the ute. He whipped up a rifle slammed a bullet into the breech and swung it in the vicinity of the pig. The runner and tusker were past the car and only a yard or two apart. They were also about to run out of light into darkness.

Once that happened Max wouldn't know where to aim for fear of hitting Kevin who had managed to identify as the man running ahead of the tusker. He had to take the shot and the last part of the pig he would still be able to see was the back legs. If he hit one then the pig would fall and skid along and it would be slowed.

He threw the rifle to his shoulder took a quick squint at the sights and pulled the trigger. The gun exploded and the pig disappeared out of the light. The entire group held their breaths and waited to hear what noise would pierce the still air.

Nothing.

The seconds ticked by then a voice from the darkness yelled, "Gee that was the closest I've ever been to a tusker in full flight"

Kevin staggered out of the dark and walked towards the group of hunters. They cheered and one said, "Who the hell fired that shot!"

"It was Max I saw him sprinting for the ute that Danielle had spun out and seconds later a shot."

Everyone was yelling their congratulations and thanks to Max who was sitting on the tray shaking like a leaf. Kevin yelled out, "Get the pigs and let's get out of here." The men picked up the carcases and returned to the utes and hung them on the side of the utes. They now had to drive to Danielle's parents' house in Wellington. This is where the pigs would be dressed ready for sale. It was imperative the convoy reached Wellington before sunrise so as to beat the pesky flies. They would swarm around and some of the carcases could get fly blown.

The old tusker had managed to flee and was by now hiding never to return. All in all, the hunters had nine piglets and one mature female.

There were also several shaken hunters and two who were slapped on their back many times for their heroic deeds.

∽o∾

At three o'clock the other hunters met up at the front gate and a quick tally showed 15 piglets, 2 sows and one tusker. It had been a successful hunt.

Danielle invited every one back to her parents' butcher shop come house in Wellington. "It's a half hours drive and we can rest up before going back to civilisation." There was laughter all round before Danielle put out the challenge, "We'll tell you about the boar's near miss as well. Come on I'll be there first so follow the dust." She wound up her window and accelerated hard. The car spun through the open gate and turned west.

Matthew Albert and his wife Freda were waiting in the kitchen for the arrival of the pig hunters. They knew that with Danielle with the men everything would go like clockwork. Right on 4 o'clock Danielle pulled up in the lane way and she burst through the side door calling, "Mum and dad we've got over a dozen so I hope that butcher's knife is honed and you two are ready to slice these carcases.

The work begun in earnest and as the minutes slipped away so did the men. They went hunting for a place to lie down and doze. A good six hours would refresh them for the trip back to Sydney.

Danielle came to Max and tapped him on the shoulders. "We'll share the hero story with everyone later. You've done enough Max, follow me."

He followed her like a little lamb and found himself in the main bedroom. "Mum said she made it up specially for us to enjoy."

The hours of sleeplessness was catching up fast on Max and much to Danielle's chagrin he was asleep before she could stir up any action. She rolled over facing away and tears ran down her cheeks.

On the trip back to St Mary's Max remained silent. This was unusual for Max but Danielle had seen this before and knew what message it carried. Danielle had even ignored the tusker story and it was left up the Kevin to thank Max and congratulate him on his fast thinking.

Matty and Joy were sitting on the steps of the blue van when the car screeched to a stop and Danielle took the swag and threw it towards Max's van. "It might be a long time before I come back, you're hopeless."

Before Max could protest or offer an excuse the car reversed through the gate and roared off back the way it had come.

Matty called out, "Hello there Max, sounds like a bit of trouble. Can we help in any way?"

Max shrugged his shoulders and picked up the swag, "Women," he said through gritted teeth, "I will never learn to understand them." He disappeared into the caravan and did not emerge until the next day.

Max had sat on the bed for a long time and he thought dark thoughts. He had had enough of Danielle and her tantrums. She harassed him all the way back from Wellington. To put on a show in front of the newcomers was unforgivable. His mind drifted to more pleasant thoughts and landed squarely with Joy.

He began to give her points in comparison to Danielle. He began with temperament and scored Joy at 10 and Danielle minus 5. Ten minutes later he totalled each woman's scores to find Danielle was a four and Joy 8.

That was now the challenge. How to turn Joy's head his way and at the same time cast Danielle out.

Max followed Joy the next day to her work place. He had been careful that she didn't know he was behind her or that may have created an awkward situation. She was now working in a Coles store as a check out chick.

He walked back to the caravan park and began to upgrade his plan. That night he invited the trio to his van for a barbeque. The meal and conversation was invigorating and as they parted Max asked Joy if he could walk her to her work tomorrow. She was at first hesitant but Edna was encouraging.

∽∘∾

The next day the two set off together to Joy's work place. Max entered the store and Joy introduced him to her boss and work mates.

The manager of the store was Ray Huntley and he began chatting to Max and they found they had many things in common. Ray was taken with Max and whenever he accompanied Joy to work or picked her up after work he found time to talk to him.

One afternoon when Max arrived at Joy's work place Ray was standing near the counter that Joy was working. He matter of factly turned to her and said, "Joy you should marry that man he is a real catch."

Joy was embarrassed by the talk of marriage and hushed Ray. Max was not privy to the exchange so nothing became of the talk.

Max and Joy's parents, as Max had decided to call them, were getting on exceptionally well. Max was considered a trustworthy friend and Joy was being allowed to go on drives with him.

Max was always the most polite and considerate person when he was with Joy. He knew that any wrong move or comment he would lose her.

Christmas was coming soon and Max agonised over what he could buy for Joy. Matty and Edna were easy to shop for as they were both keen golfers. So Max bought them a sand wedge which they both needed as in Mildura they did not have sand traps. Now that they were playing at a Sydney Golf Course they had to need for a sand wedge. All the Sydney Courses had sandtraps.

Joy was a totally different person as she was not sporty and seemed to have every clothing outfit anyone would need.

Joy accidentally helped Max out. He was talking to Matty one morning while he was fixing his car. The carburettor was sucking too much air and this caused a chugging movement as the car was driven along.

The conversation moved to pig hunting and how could Matty join a hunting group. Max was happy to offer a place the next time he was going out.

Joy walked around the corner and stopped. She was excited at the prospect of going hunting with Max and she even contemplated going with him alone. She joined in, "I would love to go hunting too. It would be a great Christmas present and something different that I've never done before."

Matty was not so keen on seeing Joy with a group of men shooting wild pigs. He said, "I don't think it is for a young lady to participate in. It can be gory at times and downright dangerous at others."

Max decided to push the idea with Matty and Edna seeing that Joy was more than happy to go with him. After a week Matty took Max aside and said, "Max we'll let Joy go with you as long as you can promise that you will not try any funny business and you will respect her. Any problems and we will pull out and you will never see her again. It is getting obvious that she is smitten by your charms but we need to consider she is very young and fragile."

Max was overjoyed and couldn't wait to ask Joy to accompany him next weekend. They would be going together and no one else.

When it comes to love Joy learnt that weekend to 'never say never'.

The pig shoot was in the Blue Mountains and was barely successful. The pair had decided to leave on the afternoon of Saturday 15th November and stay overnight. The whole family and Max had spent the morning celebrating Joy's twentieth birthday. Max cooked up a barbeque consisting of the customary sausages and steak with onion rings. This was served with tomato sauce and bread thickly buttered.

The party was non-alcoholic due to the trip into the Blue Mountains to go pig shooting.

The birthday girl and Max travelled light as it was only an overnighter. The heaviest item was the 303 rifle. The trip to the potential pig ground was relatively short and only took Max an hour to reach.

They hunted in daylight without success. As the sun set, they hooked up the spotlight and captured a sow and three piglets in its blaring light. The sow was too cunning and she veered back into the thick scrub. Max fired a shot more in frustration than any expectation of hitting the pig,

After two hours in the darkness of the night and staring into the powerful beam of the spotlight, Max stopped and set up three tins for Joy to shoot at. It was her first and definitely her last shooting of a rifle. The recoil threw her to the ground and bruised her shoulder and she missed the target by a long way. That was the end and Max knew better than to pursue such activities in the future.

Joy was embarrassed by her frivolous attempt and felt she had let Max down as he wanted her to be like Danielle. She walked to the car and climbed into the back seat, more as a habit than an invitation. Max saw the gesture in different light. Max tried ever so hard to keep his hands to himself and was shocked but delighted when Joy couldn't keep her hands to herself. They ended up in the back seat of the Pontiac madly in love and entangled in each other's bodies.

Max had left the radio tuned into the ABC and the song being broadcast at the moment they would remember for ever was,

"The Twelfth of Never" by Matty Mathis. They drifted off to the words:

> *"You ask how long I'll love you,*
> *I'll tell you true*
> *Until the twelfth of never,*
> *I'll still be loving you."*